BYSTANDER

BYSTANDER

BY JAMES PRELLER

SQUARE FISH

FEIWEL AND FRIENDS
NEW YORK, NY

Dedicated in memory of my brother John,
loving father to David and Ryan

**SQUARE
FISH**
An Imprint of Macmillan

Library of Congress Cataloging-in-Publication Data
Preller, James.
Bystander / James Preller.
p. cm.
Summary: Thirteen-year-old Eric discovers there are consequences to not
standing by and watching as the bully at his new school hurts people, but although
school officials are aware of the problem, Eric may be the one with a solution.
ISBN 978-0-312-54796-7
[1. Bullies—Fiction. 2. Conduct of life—Fiction. 3. Middle schools—Fiction.
4. Schools—Fiction. 5. Moving, Household—Fiction. 6. Divorce—Fiction.
7. Family life—New York (State)—New York—Fiction.
8. Long Island (N.Y.)—Fiction.]
I. Title. PZ7.P915Bys 2009 [Fic]—dc22 2008028554

Originally published in the United States by Feiwel and Friends
First Square Fish Edition: May 2011
Square Fish logo designed by Filomena Tuosto
mackids.com

11 13 15 17 19 20 18 16 14 12

AR: 4.2 / F&P: U / LEXILE: HL600L

Where you been is good and gone
All you keep is the gettin' there.

— Townes Van Zandt,

"To Live Is to Fly"

1

[ketchup]

THE FIRST TIME ERIC HAYES EVER SAW HIM, DAVID HALLEN-back was running, if you could call it that, running in a halting, choppy-stepped, stumpy-legged shamble, slowing down to look back over his shoulder, stumbling forward, pausing to catch his breath, then lurching forward again.

He was running *from,* not *to,* and not running, but *fleeing.*

Scared witless.

Eric had never seen the boy before. But in this town, a place called Bellport, Long Island, it was true of most kids. Eric didn't know anybody. He bounced the basketball, flicking it with his fingertips, not looking at the ball, or the rim, or anything else on the vast, empty grounds behind the middle school except for that curly-haired kid who couldn't run to save his life. Which was too bad, really, because it looked to Eric like he might be doing exactly that—running for his life.

Eric took a halfhearted jumper, missed. No lift in his legs. The ball bounced to the left wing, off the asphalt court and onto the grass, where it rolled and settled, unchased. Eric had been shooting for almost an hour. Working on his game or just killing time, Eric wasn't sure. He was tired and hot and a little bored or else he would have bounded after the ball like a pup, pounced on it after the first bounce, spun on spindly legs, and fired up a follow-up shot. Instead he let the ball roll to the grass and, hands on his hips, dripping sweat, watched the running boy as he continued across the great lawn in his direction.

He doesn't see me, Eric thought.

Behind him there was the sprawling Final Rest Pet Cemetery. According to Eric's mother, it was supposedly the third-largest pet cemetery in the United States.

And it's not like Eric's mom was making that up just to make Eric feel better about "the big move" from Ohio to Long Island. Because, duh, nobody is going to get all pumped up just because there's a big cemetery in your new hometown, stuffed with dead cats and dogs and whatever else people want to bury. Were there pet lizards, tucked into little felt-lined coffins? Vietnamese potbellied pigs? Parakeets? People were funny about pets. But burying them in a real cemetery, complete with engraved tombstones? That was a new one on Eric. A little *excessive*, he thought.

As the boy drew closer, Eric could see that his shirt was torn. Ripped along the side seam, so that it flapped as he ran. And . . . was that blood? There were dark red splotches on the boy's shirt and jeans (crazy to wear those on a hot August afternoon). Maybe it was just paint. The whole scene didn't look right, that much was sure. No one seemed to be chasing after the boy. He had come from the far side of the school and now traveled across the back of it. The boy's eyes kept returning to the corner of the building, now one hundred yards away. Nothing there. No monsters, no goblins, no ghosts, no *thing* at all.

Eric walked to his basketball, picked it up, tucked it under his arm, and stood watching the boy. He still hadn't spotted Eric, even though he was headed in Eric's direction.

At last, Eric spoke up. "You okay?" he asked. Eric's voice was soft, even gentle, but his words stopped the boy like a cannon shot to the chest. He came to a halt and stared at Eric. The boy's face was pale, freckled, mushy, with small, deep-set eyes and a fat lower lip that hung like a tire tube. He looked distrustful, a dog that had been hit by too many rolled-up newspapers.

Eric stepped forward, gestured to the boy's shirt. "Is that blood?"

The boy's face was blank, unresponsive. He didn't seem to understand.

"On your shirt," Eric pointed out.

The boy looked down, and when his eyes again lifted to meet Eric's, they seemed distant and cheerless. There was a flash of something else there, just a fleeting something in the boy's eyes: hatred.

Hot, dark hatred.

"No, no. Not . . . bl-blood," the boy said. There might have been a trace of a stutter in his voice, something in the way he paused over the "bl" consonant blend.

Whatever it was, the red glop was splattered all over the boy's pants and shirt. Eric could see traces of it in the boy's hair. Then Eric smelled it, a familiar whiff, and he knew. Ketchup. The boy was covered with ketchup.

Eric took another step. A look of panic filled the boy's eyes. He tensed, stepped back, swiveled his head to again check the far corner of the building. Then he took off without a word. He moved past Eric, beyond the court, through a gap in the fence, and into the cemetery.

"Hey!" Eric called after him. "I'm not—"

But the ketchup boy was long gone.

2

[pretty]

THEY CAME SOON AFTER, AS ERIC HAD GUESSED THEY might. Four of them on bicycles. Three boys and a girl.

Eric was alone on the court, standing at the foul line. He dribbled twice, caught the ball in both hands, feeling for the lines of the ball with his fingertips. Foul shooting was a ritual, a practiced set of precise patterns. He took a deep breath, blew the air out, bent his knees, eyes fixed on the rim. Elbow up and out, wrist flicked. The ball shivered through the mesh. Perfect.

The hunters came from around the far side of the big brick building. They weren't pedaling hard, didn't seem in any big hurry. They were talking and laughing as they rode, glancing around, the trail gone cold. Eric retrieved the ball and stepped back to the foul line. He glanced behind him, in the direction where the ketchup boy had fled. There was no sign of the boy; he had vanished like a ghost among the tombstones. That left just Eric. And now the bike riders were headed his way, four sailboats fixed on a distant shore, tacking this way and that in zigs and zags, but surely aimed toward the boy on the court in red basketball shorts, white new kicks, and a sleeveless tee.

The shaggy-haired boy in the lead pulled up right in the middle of the court, halfway between the foul line and the basket. He stayed on his bicycle seat, balanced on one leg, cool as a breeze. The boy looked at Eric. And Eric watched him look.

His hair fell around his eyes and below his ears, wavy and uncombed. He had soft features with thick lips and long eyelashes. The boy appeared to be around Eric's age, maybe a year older, and looked, well, *pretty*. It was the word that leaped into Eric's mind, and for no other reason than because it was true.

The other three stayed on their bicycles and slowly

circled the perimeter of the court, riding behind Eric and then back around and around, the noose of their circle drawing tighter each time. They, too, said nothing, as if content to wait for instructions.

Eric wondered if something bad was about to happen. And he wondered, too, if there might be anything he could do to avoid it. A part of him watched the scene unfold as if he wasn't in the middle of it, as if it was in a movie or something, as if he watched from an overhead camera, the cyclists circling like vultures around a carcass.

"You didn't see anybody come by here, did you?" the boy asked.

"Looks like a french fry," a skinny, hatchet-faced boy added. He laughed, and the third boy joined in. Eric glanced at them, avoiding eye contact, then turned to look directly back at the leader, the one who had asked the question.

"I've been shooting around," Eric explained with a shrug. "I didn't really—"

"Nobody, huh," the brown-haired boy said, sliding off his bike and dropping it carelessly to the ground.

He didn't look that big or that strong, but he moved with an easy confidence. There was toughness there, a hardness beneath the long lashes and full lips. The boy held out his hands, clapped once. Said, "Let's see that ball, huh."

Eric didn't hesitate. He made a sharp bounce pass to the boy. "Sure, here," he said, as if there was nothing he wanted more than to hand over his ball to this stranger.

The other two boys deposited their bikes on the grass. The girl—with a high, round forehead and straight blond hair parted in the middle—remained seated on her bike, wrists dangling over the handlebars, silently watching.

"You new around here?" the boy asked. He dribbled the ball a little awkwardly, his skills unrefined.

Eric nodded. Yes, he was new. Eric sensed that he'd have to be careful; this encounter could go either way. It could turn out okay, or go very bad. Threat hung in the air, though no one had said or done anything wrong. It was just a feeling Eric got. A knot in his stomach.

The boy turned to the hoop and took a shot that

clanged off the metal backboard and bounced away. He grinned and shrugged, eyes smiling. "I'm not really one of those basketball guys," he explained. "My name's Griffin. Most everybody calls me Griff."

"I'm Eric."

Griffin gestured toward the school building. "You gonna go to school here? What grade you in?"

"Yeah," Eric answered. "Seventh."

"Lucky you."

One of the other boys, the heavy, raw-knuckled one, snorted, "You any good at homework? We could use somebody to do our homework."

The hatchet-faced boy laughed. His large front teeth protruded slightly and his black hair was limp and ragged. Eric instinctively disliked him. *Weasel,* he thought.

Griffin smiled at Eric. "Don't pay any attention to these guys," he said. "They think they're funny. Anything for a laugh, right, Cody?"

The ugly one, all beaked nose and buckteeth, blew a bubble and let it burst. "Good times," he chirped. "Good times."

"I feel sorry for you," Griffin said to Eric. "You

move here—and all *we've* been trying to do is figure out how to *break out* of this place!"

Griffin had a way about him, a certain kind of natural leadership that Eric respected. Words came easily to Griffin, his smile was bright and winning. Eric felt almost envious; Griffin seemed to possess a quality he lacked, a *presence*.

"So, tell us," Griffin continued, commanding the court. "Why did you move here?"

"Well, it wasn't my idea," Eric confessed. "My parents . . . sort of . . ."

He trailed off. Better keep that part to himself.

"You don't talk a lot, do you," Griff noted.

Eric tilted his head, shrugged, embarrassed.

"He's a shy boy!" the big one squealed.

"Shut up, Drew P.," Griff said. "Get me that ball, will ya?"

And Drew P. did.

"Droopy, Droo-pee," Cody chimed in a mocking, singsong voice.

"Get a life," Droopy snapped back.

Griffin shook his head, as if the dialogue disappointed him. He explained to Eric, "His name is Drew

Peterson. The other day we started calling him 'Droop' and 'Droopy.' Get it: *Drew P.*" Griffin smiled. "I don't think he's crazy about it."

Eric didn't respond, just listened and nodded.

Griffin weighed the ball in one hand. "You mind if we keep this?"

"What?"

"The ball, Eric," Griffin said. "You don't mind if I keep it for a while, do you? As a souvenir?"

"Yep, yep, yep!" Cody chirped.

Eric started to answer. "I, um—"

"Um . . . what?" Griffin interrupted, his face a mask now, hard to read. "You think maybe you have a choice?"

The two other boys moved a little closer to Eric, one on each side. They seemed to grow in stature. A little taller, a little fiercer, the way a dog looks when its hackles are raised.

Eric did the math. Three against one, not counting the girl. She wasn't doing anything, just standing by, watching.

No, no choice, Eric thought. *No choice at all.*

3
[joking]

HE DID NOT WANT TO PART WITH HIS BASKETBALL. BUT Eric knew that if he caved right now, just a week before school started, he'd be a marked man for the whole year. It was funny, almost. School hadn't begun, but he was already taking his first test.

"Actually, um, I *do* mind," Eric finally said. He didn't whine it or say it with a whimper. He just told it flat out. The sky was blue, the grass was green, and he would certainly miss the damn ball. "But you guys can play with it," Eric quickly added. "I mean, I was about to head home in a few minutes, but—"

Griffin laughed out loud. "Dude, hey, we're just busting on you." He passed the ball back to Eric, a one-handed fling. "I don't even like basketball."

"Come on, Griff, let's go. I'm bored."

It was the girl.

She said, "It's too hot. Let's find Sinjay and get invited into his pool."

Griffin looked at her, nodded once. "Yeah, I guess." He turned back to Eric. "So," he said, landing on the word with emphasis, like it was a complete thought, a summarizing statement. So. "You *really* didn't see a kid come through here? For sure?"

Eric looked him in the eye and blinked. "I'm just shooting around. I'm like in my own little world out here."

"Okay, I'll take your word for it." Griffin looked around, slowly rubbed his hand across his chest and belly.

Eric could see the doubt in Griffin's eyes. He volunteered, "I mean, I think I would have noticed somebody if—"

"I gotcha," Griffin replied, sharp and dismissive. "Loud and clear. You didn't see him. Nothing wrong with that. We're just looking for one of our buddies, that's all. You can understand that, can't you?"

Eric said that he could.

Griffin's face brightened. "Hey, I've got an idea," he said, snapping his fingers. "This will be really fun, Eric. You will definitely enjoy it. We'll give you one shot, from right there"—he pointed at the foul line—"and if you make it, you get to keep the basketball. If you miss"—he shrugged—"we take it."

"Sounds like a plan," Drew P. said.

"Yep, yep, yep!" Cody called out. That's when Eric recognized the voice. Cody was doing a pitch-perfect imitation of Petrie from *The Land Before Time*. Eric's younger brother, Rudy, had spent a full year obsessed with those videos.

"Come *on*, Griff," the girl persisted. "This is so lame."

Eric considered his options. There weren't any good ones. "Okay," he relented. "One shot. But what do I get if I make it?"

"Ho-ho!" Griffin exclaimed. "Now you're bargaining, huh? I like that, Eric, very ballsy."

"I bet a dollar he makes it," the girl said.

"I'll take that bet," Cody said.

Griffin eyed her appraisingly, eyebrows arched in mock surprise. "You like the looks of him, huh? The new boy in town?"

She made an "oh, please" face, like the very idea was stupid. "Let's just get this over with, Griff."

So Eric dribbled once, twice, took a deep breath, and laid a brick. He missed everything, the backboard, the rim, the works. His heart sank.

"Air ball!" chortled Drew P.

"You owe me a dollar, Mary!" Cody claimed.

Mary. Her name was Mary.

Griffin grabbed the ball. He set it on the ground, rested his foot on it, stood pondering the possibilities, then gently rolled the ball to Eric.

Eric bent to pick it up and murmured, "Thanks." The word slipped past his lips as a reflex, just tumbled off his tongue without thinking, a verbal somersault of ingrained manners, *thanks*, and Eric kicked himself for saying it. What an idiot. Thanking these guys for *not* stealing his ball! Actually *thanking* them! How pathetic.

"I am disappointed in you, Eric. I really thought

you'd make that shot," Griffin said. He lifted his bike off the ground, climbed back onto it. "We'll see you in school, Eric. Who knows? Maybe we'll have a few classes together. Wouldn't that be special? We could go to the library and do homework together!" He let out a friendly laugh, like it was all a big fat joke.

"Yeah," Eric replied.

The gang of four pulled away. Griffin gestured toward the pet cemetery, and they headed for a gap in the fence.

Eric let out a deep breath. He felt the tension seep out of his neck and shoulders. *Good riddance,* he thought. No wonder his shot fell short. Too stressed. The girl, Mary, was right. It was hotter than hell out here.

Eric didn't hear Griffin's return, not until the boy was almost on top of him.

"Hey, man," Griffin said, startling Eric as he pulled up behind him, back tire skidding. The others hadn't followed. It was just Eric and Griffin now, no one else. "I don't want you getting the wrong idea. You know we're just fooling around, right? I was never going to take your ball or anything like that."

"I know," Eric said.

"Because you looked a little worried there for a minute." Griffin laughed.

"No, no," Eric protested. "I knew you were just having fun."

Griffin flashed a smile, that hundred-dollar smile he could turn on in an instant. He reached out his fist. "Are we cool, buddy?"

Eric tapped his fist against Griffin's.

"Sure."

"Welcome to Bellport," Griffin said, lifting both hands, arms out wide. "You ever need anything, anybody ever gives you trouble, you just come find me. My name is Griffin Connelly. Everybody knows me. I'll watch out for you. Okay?"

Eric nodded.

"I'm a good guy to be friends with," Griffin said. He placed a firm hand on Eric's shoulder. "But I'm a lousy enemy."

Eric had already figured as much.

"Maybe we'll hang out someday, I'll show you around town," Griffin offered. "Of course, it will take all of five minutes, because there's nothing to do around here. By the way," he said, leaning in close, "my friend Mary, she said you were cute."

Griffin grinned and gave Eric a knowing, heavy-lidded leer. Then he rose up on his pedal and rode away.

4

[fresh]

HIS MOM HAD CALLED IT A NEW BEGINNING. SHE SAID HE should think of it as a fresh start. Those were her exact words, like she had memorized them from some drugstore greeting card. "You're just going to have to trust me on this," she said.

Well, what do you say to that? So Eric nodded, looked at the floor, and said, "Sure, sure, sure." Yes, he trusted her; yes, he loved her; yes, yes, a thousand times, yes. What did she want from him? Rainbows and unicorns?

So she sold the house, Eric said good-bye to his

friends, and the fractured family headed east. They drove in a car behind a rental truck through Maryland and Pennsylvania, into New Jersey and New York, and finally across the Throgs Neck Bridge and onto Long Island. His brave new world.

Bellport was his mom's old hometown. She still had a few friends there, from back in the day. The support she claimed she needed; and, most important, the promise of a good job selling medical supplies for some big company. "*Bueno* bucks," she commented. Plus, his mother confessed, "I always missed the ocean when we lived in Ohio." The salty Atlantic. There was even a bicycle path you could take all the way to the Jones Beach boardwalk. She couldn't wait to smell that briny breeze again.

Eric didn't care. And it was getting harder to pretend he did.

The way he figured it, there was no such thing as a new beginning. You get one life and it rolls out like a long hallway carpet. It begins on the day you are born and keeps on rolling until you drop. There's no refresh button, no start-over option. At night when he was alone in bed, that's when Eric felt it the most.

Fooling nobody, not even himself, no matter how hard he tried. Eric missed his dad and he couldn't stop thinking about it.

Not lonely, but worse: alone, abandoned.

He promised himself that if he ever saw that man again, Eric would turn his back and walk away. See how he liked it. Stick in the knife and give it a twist.

Eric had seen other families break up. He got that part of it. He just didn't want it to happen to *his* family. And definitely not the *way* it happened, with his dad flaking out. Lots of dads moved out. But usually they bought a house in the next town, or an apartment down the road. They had weekend visits, dinners at lonely Italian restaurants on Wednesday nights, coached Little League, and bankrolled big summer vacations. Not Eric's dad. He just lost it, stopped going to work, stopped functioning, and eventually just dropped out of sight. Gone, Daddy, gone. He left and never came back, even though he kept saying he *would*—or was it that he *might*?

His mom said that his father went off looking for something, as if he were searching for a lost lottery ticket. "He'll be back," she used to promise. "He's just struggling right now," she said. "It's not his fault." But weeks became months, the months became years, and his father never found it, that missing something. He never showed up again, either. Which led them to Bellport and the necessity of "a fresh new start," like Eric's actual life was some kind of "new and improved" fabric softener.

How does a father do that? Just screw up everything?

He sent CDs, though. That was the big joke. Every once in a while, a padded envelope arrived in his father's handwriting addressed to Eric. He made these random CDs, mostly filled with classic rock, stuff like Creedence Clearwater Revival and Bob Dylan and the Allman Brothers, music the dinosaurs used to listen to back in the Jurassic, songs he felt Eric might like. And he was mostly right about that; the tunes were pretty good. His father phoned sometimes, too, but never seemed to say anything. It was like he was in a fog, his thoughts confused. He just wasn't the same man anymore.

For sure, he never said the one thing Eric wanted to hear.

He never said, "I'm better now. I'm coming home."

Some dad, huh? Just swell.

He called yesterday. Eric didn't even know why. It was a question he kept wanting to ask, if he had the courage: "Why you calling, Dad? What's the point?"

The phone got passed around from his mother to his little brother, Rudy, and finally to Eric. The conversation was brief and awkward. As if his father was tired, talked out.

Eric kept thinking of it this way: It was like his father was a great bird that had flown away, and all Eric could do was watch that bird drift into the distance, smaller, smaller, until it seemed to vanish completely, lost in the clouds. It felt a little like death, a wisp of smoke vanishing in the air, gone but not forgotten.

So, okay, the phone calls didn't go real well.

Or maybe Eric just wasn't very nice.

"You probably hate me," his father observed.

Eric didn't answer. He recognized the code. He knew it was really a question, a desperate request, and he heard the ache behind it. The answer his father was looking for was something like "Oh no, Daddy. Don't worry about us! You're still the World's Greatest Dad!" Like on those coffee mugs you see at the mall, the lamest Father's Day gift ever.

But Eric wasn't a little kid anymore. Not like Rudy. He was thirteen years old. Lucky thirteen. Try to roll that with a pair of dice. And the truth was, Eric just didn't have it to give. A part of him had been ripped out like the stuffing from a pillow. So Eric remained silent on the phone. Kept his father waiting. If Eric listened very hard, he could almost hear his father twisting in the wind, the groan of the rope. A little revenge that didn't make Eric feel any better.

"I guess that's it," his father said. "You don't have to say anything, Eric. I'm sorry—I'm so sorry. I just can't. I can't."

Click, and he was gone, again. Call over.

Eric looked at the phone in his hand, shot daggers at his mom, snapped it shut. He went into the kitchen, looked for something to eat. A bowl of Rice Krispies, some pretzels, anything.

His mother barked something about dinner being almost ready, and not to spoil his appetite. Rag, rag, rag. So he grabbed his iPod instead, slid open the back door, and parked himself in a lawn chair. Eric turned the music up, let it pour into him, fill him up. He had downloaded the songs from his dad's CDs. Eric did not curse, or cry, or seem to feel much of anything. It was all just a swirling mass, a crazy mess inside his numb skull. He closed his eyes and heard Led Zeppelin guitarist Jimmy Page pick out the first notes of "Communication Breakdown," rapid-fire like a machine gun on the open E string, before hitting three big chords, D-A-D. Then singer Robert Plant's siren wail: "Hey, girl, stop what you're doin'!"

It had rained and some worms crawled from their holes out onto the brick patio. Eric grabbed a stick and idly poked at one, turning it over. That's how he felt, he decided. Just like that worm. Pushed around, prodded by a stick. After a while he'd crawl back into his hole. And then, in a few days, off to school. A new hole with red bricks and homework.

It would be a fresh start. A new beginning. Isn't that what his mom said? New and improved. Guaranteed or your money back.

5

[school]

BELLPORT CENTRAL MIDDLE SCHOOL INCLUDED GRADES six to eight, with students streaming in from four different elementary schools. It was organized into "houses"—like at Hogwarts, Eric noted, but without the exploding jelly beans or cool wizard tricks—and somehow that was supposed to make the experience more manageable. Unfortunately, as they say, timing is everything, and it was plain bad luck that Eric arrived a year too late, after the newness of sixth had hardened into established groups. By seventh grade everybody knew one another. Routines had been set, cliques formed. But Eric was ready for that. He'd be all right. It was just going to take some time, that's all.

Eric rode his bike to school that first day, while his younger brother watched TV at home, still in his pajamas. The elementary school didn't start until an hour later. Eric pulled up to the bike rack a few minutes early, as a long row of buses disgorged a torrent of students. They poured into the main lobby like a babbling river, to resounding shouts and waves and chatter. When he climbed the front steps and entered the building, Eric was immersed in a roiling sea of faces. The noise, the tumult, the clatter! Eric brushed up against soap-scrubbed girls wearing strawberry lip balm, pushed past boys whose armpits were slathered with sickly-smelling antiperspirant. It was the first minute of the first day of school, a time of hope and electricity. Sure, everyone would soon be complaining about dull teachers and too much homework, but for these first few seconds, it was all promise and possibility.

The kids in Bellport didn't seem much different from the ones Eric knew back in Ohio. Maybe they appeared better dressed, a little trendier; they had more money, snazzy cell phones, probably their own laptops. The girls wore more makeup, had complicated haircuts, walked with more swish and swagger. Eric wasn't sure if that was a difference between Long Island and Ohio, or just part of growing up. By the looks of things, some of these girls had grown plenty. A few of them seemed years older than Eric, and pretty intimidating.

Eric's big fear on the first day was getting lost. And BCMS was the perfect school for it, a vast, sprawling maze of hallways. Over the summer Eric had received a packet of information designed for incoming students that included his schedule, a letter from the principal (which he ignored), a sixteen-page curriculum guide (tossed aside), and a map (memorized). Each day he took out the map alongside his schedule, and traced a finger along the best routes. He didn't like the idea of going in without a plan. Eric liked to come prepared. It must have been all those camping trips he used to take with the Boy Scouts. Back when his father still tried to act like a normal dad. The meals, the clothes, everything planned down to the last detail. Now Eric had a real good idea where he was going.

The first two periods—math and science—were

decent enough. Eric thought it was good to get those tough subjects out of the way first thing in the morning, before he was really awake. Then he'd breeze through the easier classes in the middle of the day, like PE and art, not to mention lunch and home base, before ending his day with two of his favorites, social studies and English.

Home base was where he was headed now, at 9:52 in the morning. The hallways pulsed with life. Behind him he heard a body slam into a locker, a muffled *oomph*, and the splatter of books falling to the floor.

"Body check!" a voice announced.

"Hallenback," scolded another voice, "watch where you're going, buddy. You're gonna be late for class."

"Yep, yep, yep!" chirped another voice.

Eric didn't turn around, didn't glance back. He kept right on walking, distancing himself from the sound of laughter and the voices of Griffin Connelly and that other one, the Weasel.

6

[hallenback]

HOME BASE WAS A BIG DEAL AT BCMS. MR. SCOFIELD, Eric's home base and English teacher, began the period by calling it "the lynchpin of the middle school experience."

Um, sure.

"What's a lynchpin?" a girl asked.

Mr. Scofield considered the question. "Have you ever seen any old Westerns on TV? You know those old covered wagons from *Little House on the Prairie*? Well, they used to put in a pin crosswise through the axle to keep the wheel from coming off. That's called a lynchpin. It keeps everything rolling along!"

Eric noted that approximately six people were listening to Mr. Scofield, and half seemed to regret it. Undeterred, the bald-shaven teacher continued, "A lynchpin is an essential element in the success of a team or a plan. That's home base."

In other words, as Eric figured it, home base was a free period, except you weren't exactly free. But students were allowed to read or study what they wanted, catch up on homework, talk quietly, hang out. They could even go visit with other teachers, or get passes to the library if they showed they were working on special projects. They didn't hand out "Get Out of Jail Free" cards, but it was the next best thing.

The girl who Eric recognized from the other day sashayed into the room a few minutes late. *Mary,* he remembered. She nodded at Mr. Scofield, mumbled something about a jammed locker, and took a seat in the back.

"Let's not make this a habit, Miss O'Malley."

"No, sir," she answered.

Eric turned to watch her. If Mary saw him, or

cared in the least, she didn't give any sign of it. She was already saying hello to a few other girls, quickly engrossed in conversation.

When he glanced back at Mary, Eric noticed a semi-familiar face, like a boy who looked like somebody he once knew. Eric caught the boy peering at him sideways, a little hunched in his chair, head low, books a jumbled mess, binder open. Every time Eric looked up, he seemed to catch that kid staring at him. It was irritating. But then Eric remembered that day on the basketball court, and the boy running to the pet cemetery. Here he saw that same pale, freckled face. He had curly hair and wore a wounded, wary expression.

That's him, Eric realized. *Ketchup boy. He remembers me.*

Eric gave him a nod, an almost imperceptible chin lift. A look of hostility flickered across the boy's face— a flash of anger, bright as a naked lightbulb—then he turned away, stared at the book on his desk. Eric understood immediately. The boy was embarrassed, shamed. And Eric, as witness to that shame, was a party to it. Innocent or not, *he was there.*

Eric learned the boy's name during attendance. David Hallenback. Eric had heard that name before. Yes, he remembered: the crash against the locker, the mocking voice, "*Hallenback!*"

It appeared that Griffin Connelly was right. He did make a lousy enemy.

No matter what happened in the future, or how their lives might come to intersect, Eric would think of Hallenback as forever shambling across that field, haunted and hunted; no matter what else happened, Eric would envision Hallenback as he was revealed that singular summer afternoon—covered in ketchup, covered in shame.

"I wouldn't talk to that kid if I was you." Eric turned and she was there, sitting in the chair beside him.

Brown-eyed Mary O'Malley.

"What?"

Mary smiled at him. Tilted her head toward Hallenback. "Him," she said. "You should stay away. If you are nice to him even once, you'll never get rid of him. It's like feeding a stray dog."

Mary wore jeans and a loose shirt, no makeup, but still looked tanned and athletic. "You were with those guys that day," he noted.

"I was with Griff," she said. "We sometimes hang out. The others were just sort of there."

Eric glanced back at Hallenback, who was observing them while pretending to read. "That's the kid you guys were chasing, right?"

Eric instantly regretted his mistake, wished he could take back the words. On the basketball court, he had told Griff that he didn't see anyone.

Mary stretched, languidly raising her arms in the air. Her eyes coolly assessed Eric, studying him. "So you lied, huh? I knew it."

"I didn't want to get involved," Eric explained.

"Sure."

"Did he do something wrong?"

Mary leaned forward. "I'm just telling you, because you're new here, and you seem like you might be all right. Just steer clear."

"Considering the way he looks at me, that's not going to be a problem. I don't think he likes me," Eric said. He paused, watched Mary watch him, and changed his tune. "Okay, I got the message. I won't feed the stray dog. Thanks for the heads-up."

Mary stood, without hurry, to rejoin her friends in the back of the room. "What's your screen name? Do you IM?"

"IM?"

"Instant message," Mary replied.

"Oh, right! Sure, yeah," Eric bluffed. The last thing he wanted to admit was that his mother didn't allow him to use instant message. Not until he was sixteen. It was another one of her rules. Semi-flustered, Eric spluttered, "I mean, I don't IM a super lot, but—"

Mary's brown eyes smiled. "You don't have a clue, do you?"

"Not really, no," Eric admitted.

"Just give me your e-mail address," she said. "We'll go from there."

7

[lunch]

THE PROBLEM WITH THE CAFETERIA WAS THIS: WHERE DO you sit? Eric hadn't really thought about it until he stood there, food tray in his hands, inspecting the landscape. The room was huge, filled with rows of long tables. Even at a glance, Eric could guess the personalities of some of the tables: the jocks, the geeks, the popular girls, and so on.

So where did Eric fit in? Nowhere.

In class, you took a seat and sat there while the teacher rambled on. It wasn't a big lifestyle decision. But here in the lunchroom, there was no avoiding the reality that Eric didn't have a single friend in town. He was alone and he didn't want to be.

In a month, he assured himself, everything would be fine. He'd make new friends, sit with them, eat, joke, laugh. But right now, today, the first day of school, it all kind of sucked. But on another level, none of it really mattered. Eric could smell his meatball sub and he felt hungry. He wanted to eat. There was nothing complicated about that. So without thinking further, he grabbed a chair at the vacant end of a long table.

A few minutes later, he heard a voice: "Dude, tell me you are not sitting all alone at this table?" Eric looked up. It was Griffin Connelly, standing at Eric's left elbow.

"Remember me?" Griffin said, shaggy hair falling into his eyes.

Eric pointed a plastic spork at him. "Yeah, you look a little familiar," he feebly joked.

"Come on, sit with us," Griffin offered.

Eric hesitated.

"Let's go." Griffin turned and walked to the back of the room. Eric had no choice but to follow.

"Slide over, Cody," Griffin told the lank-haired,

weasel-faced boy that Eric remembered from the basketball court. "Eric's gonna sit there."

"No, it's okay," Eric protested. "I can sit over—"

"Just sit there, okay?" Griffin insisted. "It's the first
day of school. You're the new kid. And you already
look kind of pathetic. We're trying to be friendly here."
He stared at Cody, who reluctantly got up to vacate his
seat.

Griffin blew the hair out of his eyes. "So," he said
to Eric.

Eric waited for more, but there wasn't any. He
looked around the table. He saw another face he recognized, Drew P., and nodded.

"S'up," Droopy murmured, then capped it off
with a yawn.

Griffin rattled off a bunch of names—Sinjay, Will,
Hakeem, Marshall, Pat—introducing Eric to the rest
of the table. Eric nodded at everybody and got drowsy
grunts in return.

"So," Griffin began again. "What do you think of
Bellport Central Middle School so far?"

Eric shrugged, eyeballed his lunch. "The meatballs
look a little—"

"Disgusting?" Griffin suggested. "Soggy? Green? Inedible?"

Eric laughed, pushed his tray aside. He was hungry—but not *that* hungry. "It's not so bad here, really."

Griffin frowned like he knew better, but didn't bother to disagree.

"Middle school," Griffin repeated. "Where did they come up with that, anyway? We're in the middle of what, exactly? Too old for elementary school, but not big enough for high school. So they shove us here. Look around. There's not an interesting person in sight, just a bunch of clones who want to be like everybody else."

Eric nodded thoughtfully, signaling agreement. He kept his true thoughts to himself. He wasn't prepared to pass judgment on everyone in the school.

Something caught Griffin's eye and he smiled to a lunch aide as she passed behind Eric. "Hello, Mrs. Rosen," he said in a cheerful voice. "How was your summer?"

"Oh, hello, Griffin," the woman replied.

She was an older woman with black hair, around

fifty, small and trim and tidy, and she reminded Eric of a kindly mouse. She seemed pleased to see Griffin Connelly. There was genuine warmth in her voice.

"You are getting so big," she noted.

Ugh, every grown-up said that. Eric shot a look at Griffin, watching for his response.

"Eating my Wheaties!" Griffin replied, flexing his muscles and smiling. "How's that dog of yours? What's her name again?"

"Daisy," Mrs. Rosen replied. Then her face changed, the smile dropped, and she looked ten years older. "I'm afraid we had to put Daisy down."

"Oh, too bad," Griffin said, putting on a sympathetic face. "Daisy was a great little dog."

And so the conversation continued, the older lady conversing with dear, sweet Griffin Connelly. To Eric, there was something false in Griffin's tone. Too cheerful, too sweet: the wrong note. For ninety seconds, Griffin Connelly became the most polite, mild-mannered boy in Bellport. Strange.

When she walked away, Griffin smirked at Eric. "That old git's loaded," he said. "I'm telling you, she has more money than Oprah. She lives around the block from me; I've done some odd jobs for her in the past. You should have seen that little dog of hers, Eric. It was one of those—what do you call 'em?—lapdogs that just barked and barked and barked. Stupid animal. I'm glad it's dead. The world is a better place."

Eric didn't know what to say to that.

"Hey, Cody!" Griffin called down the table. "I'm still hungry. You see Hallenback around?"

Cody craned his long neck, made a quick survey of the room. He shook his head no. "You want me to try to hunt him down, Griff?" he offered.

"Don't bother, we'll catch him later," Griffin replied. He reached across the table and poured out a handful of Eric's chips. "I'll just share with my new buddy."

8

[charmed]

MRS. HAYES DECLARED THAT SATURDAY WAS ERRANDS day, and insisted on dragging along Eric and Rudy. It was her notion of "family time." Eric knew enough not to complain—much. First they found an Office Max on the never-ending strip mall of Sunrise Highway. They walked the aisles until they filled a shopping cart with school supplies. Mrs. Hayes read aloud the list that Rudy's second-grade teacher provided. Besides the usual stuff, Rudy's teacher asked each student to bring in antibacterial soap, a box of cotton balls, and three boxes of Kleenex.

"That's just stupid," Eric commented.

Rudy pouted. He didn't think so.

His mother threw a box of cotton balls into the cart. "Change your attitude," she told Eric.

They ate lunch at Friendly's.

"How come the pictures on the menu look so much better than the real food?" Rudy wondered.

"It's called advertising," Eric told his little brother. "They try to trick you into buying the frozen clams casino. You'd be better off sucking on the menu."

Rudy laughed.

"Oh, Eric, please," his mother scolded.

"What?" Eric demanded. "I'm just teaching him about—"

"You're being obnoxious," his mother snapped. "I don't know what's the matter with you today. You are so grumpy and rude. Is this the way it's going to be now that you're a teenager? I don't know if I can take your mood swings."

Thankfully, Rudy spilled his Fribble, and that took the heat off Eric. "Can we go home now?" he asked.

"No. We still have to go food shopping."

Eric grumbled. Rudy begged for Cap'n Crunch and

raspberry Fruit Roll-Ups. The twerp actually *liked* supermarkets.

The shopping only took forever, what with his mother squeezing and sniffing every melon in the produce section. On their way out of the supermarket, Eric ran into Griffin Connelly. Or to be more accurate, *almost* ran into him—with the shopping cart. Eric was pushing the overloaded, squeaky-wheeled contraption, with his mother and brother chattering along behind, when he nearly crashed into Griffin. He was standing just outside the exit doors, dressed in jeans and a white T-shirt, hands shoved deep into his pockets and leaning with one foot against the brick wall. Griffin was looking away, and for a moment Eric hoped they'd escape unnoticed. He didn't want to be seen here, not with his mother. But when Griffin glimpsed Eric, he popped off the wall and smiled like he'd just won a race. "Eric!" he exclaimed.

"Oh, hi," Eric said. He gave a subtle wave, lifting a few fingers off the cart handle. Real low-key.

Griffin extended his hand to Mrs. Hayes. "You must be Eric's mother. My name is Griffin Connelly. I go to school with Eric. We sit together at lunch."

"Well, I'm pleased to meet you," Mrs. Hayes purred, and it was perfectly true. She *was* pleased. Griffin was a good-looking kid, confident and self-assured. He had nice manners and an undeniable charm.

"Is this your little brother?" Griffin asked, tussling Rudy's hair.

"I'm not so little," Rudy retorted, pushing away Griffin's hand.

"Yow, fierce," Griffin joked, looking from Rudy to Eric to Mrs. Hayes. He was flashing the full thirty-two-tooth smile, his pearly whites gleaming like a toothpaste commercial.

Eric stood and watched, vaguely uneasy.

"Are you here with your parents?" Mrs. Hayes inquired.

"No, no," Griffin answered. He looked around, dipped his head, and confessed, "It's kind of embarrassing, actually. The truth is—this is sort of what I do every Saturday. Not too exciting, huh? I come here to help old people with their packages. They know I'll be here."

Eric's mother was charmed. "That's wonderful."

Griffin smiled beatifically. "It's hard for old people," he continued. "I think of my own grandmother and how tough it is for her to get around. I think that, you know, if I help an old lady here, maybe somebody will be nice to my grammy. She lives upstate."

Eric watched his mother's reaction, half expecting her to adopt Griffin on the spot. It was as if he had sprouted wings and now floated on a white puffy cloud. The only things missing were the harp and the halo. *Griffin Connelly, angel on this earth*. Still, Eric had to hand it to Griff. He was a smooth operator.

"Sometimes I get tips," Griffin confided. He imitated an old woman leaning on an imaginary cane. He held out a trembling hand and warbled in a crackly voice, "This quarter is for you, young man. Don't spend it all in one place."

Rudy laughed, eyes twinkling.

"Aw, that's sweet," Mrs. Hayes cooed.

Eric shifted on his feet. He was totally ready for this little chitchat to conclude.

"Hey, Eric, you should stay and hang out—if you want?" Griffin offered.

"No, I, um," Eric stammered. He jerked a thumb toward the parking lot. "My mom—we have to—"

"I think it's a wonderful idea," Mrs. Hayes chimed in. She was delighted to see that Eric made a new friend—and such a nice boy. "It's no problem," she said. "I'll bring the packages home with Rudy. We'll be fine. You can call us when you're ready to be picked up." She fished into her bag. "Here, I'll let you borrow my cell phone."

"Are you sure that—"

Griffin put an arm around Eric's shoulders and squeezed. "Thanks, Mrs. Hayes. We'll see you later. But first, let us help you with those packages. . . ."

9

[gum]

"THAT WAS SOME PERFORMANCE," ERIC COMMENTED AFter they finished loading the groceries into the car.

Griffin brought a hand to his chest in mock surprise. "What? Me? I can't help it if all the moms are crazy about me." He waved at the departing car.

"You laid it on pretty thick," Eric noted.

Griffin grinned, blew on his fingernails. "My secret weapon. It's called charm, my friend. Just watch and learn."

Griffin led Eric from the parking lot back to the

supermarket, where they lingered near the exit doors. To Eric's surprise, Griffin ignored several people who could have used assistance. Finally, he gave Eric a nudge. "Locking in on target. Set phasers on stun. Here we go."

When the automatic door opened, an older woman moved unsteadily forward, steering a shopping cart. "Mrs. Chavez!" Griffin exclaimed, smiling cheerfully. "Please, let me help you with that. . . ."

Eric had to admit it. Griffin surprised him. Together they helped four different women with their groceries. Griffin was the talker, the charmer. Eric did most of the hauling. Maybe Griffin was a little over the top, but the ladies all seemed pleased with his attentions. Twice, Griffin refused payment. "I couldn't possibly accept your money." He waved away the offer of a tip. "Helping you is payment enough."

"I see you've been raised right," one of the women observed.

"Amen," Griffin announced. He cast a glimpse heavenward, like a slugger who'd just hit one over the fence. Then he glanced at Eric and winked.

It was all a little confusing. But Eric enjoyed hanging out with Griffin, mostly. He was a smart guy, quick-witted, and he told funny stories about different teachers at school.

"What's with your friend Cody?" Eric asked. "The one who always says, 'Yep, yep, yep!' "

"What do you mean?"

"With that face of his, he reminds me of a weasel."

Griff gave him the fish eye—cold, flat, lifeless— and Eric instantly regretted his words. *Dumb, dumb, dumb.* Cody was Griffin's friend.

"I mean . . ." Eric's voice drifted off. He decided it would be better if he stopped talking altogether.

Griffin blew the hair out of his eyes, looked away. Finally he said, "Yeah, okay, a weasel. I can see that. Or a ferret." But he added a warning, "Just don't let Cody ever hear you say that. He may look scrawny, but I've seen him kick some serious butt."

"Really?"

"American Combat Karate," Griffin intoned. "He's got three older brothers and they all take lessons from a guy in town. He teaches when he's not in prison."

Eric vowed, right then and there, to never again utter the word "weasel."

Griffin suggested they go to his house. "It's only two blocks away."

"I don't know." Eric hesitated.

"Dude, what are you going to do instead? Go home and play Battleship with your little brother?"

"You have a point," Eric admitted. It was the first time he'd been invited over anybody's house since they moved to Bellport. Even if there was something *off* about Griffin, he was nonetheless friendly and entertaining. It felt good to hang out with somebody, anybody. And Griffin was obviously one of the more popular guys in school.

"Want some gum?" Griffin offered as he kicked a small rock down the street. "Here, take the whole box. I don't really like Chiclets. You can't blow bubbles."

"Then why'd you buy it?"

Griffin shrugged. "The box was there."

"I don't get it." Eric popped two pieces of gum into his mouth.

"I found the box on Mrs. Chavez's dashboard, okay, so I snagged it," Griffin confessed. He watched Eric closely, then quickly added, "Don't get all stressed. It's not like she'll miss it. That lady's got plenty of money, believe me. People like that wake up and crap hundred-dollar bills, while the rest of us . . ."

He didn't finish the sentence, so the words hung in the air like half-filled helium balloons. *The rest of us . . . what?* Eric wondered.

"We carried eight bags," Griffin reminded Eric. "A little gum is the least old Chavez can give us. We earned it. Nothing wrong with that."

"I guess," Eric said, though he didn't think so. But still, it was only gum. He asked, "Then why do you turn down tips?"

"It's about building trust," Griffin explained. "I mean, what are they going to give me? A freaking dollar? A handful of crusty nickels and dimes? Trust is worth more than chump change, Eric—way more. It's like holding a winning lottery ticket. You just have to wait for the right time before cashing it in."

10
[friend]

THERE WAS NOBODY HOME AT GRIFFIN'S HOUSE.

"I thought you said your father would be here," Eric said.

"He works weird hours," Griffin explained. "When I left, he was zonked out on that couch right there. He's probably out getting hammered, watching college football at the Tiki Bar and Grill. We're better off without him, believe me."

"What about your mother?"

"She's away for a while . . . on a trip," Griffin answered vaguely. "My older sisters moved out last year.

They don't even come visit anymore, not that I blame them. We've got the house to ourselves."

"I should check in with my mom," Eric said.

"Hey, don't let me stop you."

"She's not going to like that your folks aren't here," Eric warned.

"So lie," Griffin suggested.

"Lie?"

Griffin held his thumb and index finger a hair's breadth apart. "A little white lie," he said. "What are you? The good fairy?"

Eric made a face and dialed. "Hi, Mom."

"Hey, sweetie. Do you need me to pick you up?"

"No, we, um, that's why I'm calling," Eric explained. "We decided to hang out at Griffin's house."

"What are you going to do over there?"

"Do?" Eric looked at Griffin, who made a few waves of his hand. Eric cracked a smile. "Ping-Pong."

"Well, I don't have a problem with it. Are his parents home?"

"His parents?" Eric looked to Griffin, who signaled a thumbs-up. "Yes," Eric said. "Mr. Connelly's here."

"Great, may I speak with him?"

"You want to speak with him?" Eric echoed. He looked at Griffin, who tilted his head up, began scrubbing his armpits, pretended to wash his hair. "He's, um, I think he's in the—he's showering!" Eric said.

"Showering, huh?" Mrs. Hayes paused a beat, giving Eric's heart time to climb into his throat.

"I can ask him to call you later," he offered.

"No, I have to run out," Mrs. Hayes answered. "Rudy has been invited to a bowling party. Can you believe that kid? One month in town and he's already Mr. Popularity. Besides, you have my cell, remember? If you get home before me, I want you to do something constructive."

"Mom—"

"I mean it. No TV, no electronics. Read a book, clean your room, practice your guitar. We'll be home around five."

"You know, Mom," Eric said, seizing the opening, "this is why I need my own cell phone."

He heard her sigh. "Maybe you're right, I don't know. We'll talk about it later. Love you."

Eric glanced at Griffin. "You, too."

And that was that. In one quick call, Eric had lied

to his mother. He had to, he reasoned, or she would have never let him stay at Griffin's house. It wasn't like they were going to do anything bad.

"Your mother's old school, huh?" Griffin noted.

"I guess so, if that means super-strict."

"Don't sweat it," Griffin advised. "You did good. She'll never know the difference. No harm, no foul."

Eric nodded, shrugged it off as no big deal. "I don't suppose you even *have* a Ping-Pong table, do you?"

Griffin laughed, held his wrists out in front of his body. "I confess, Officer. You caught me. Go ahead, slap on the 'cuffs, haul me off to the Big House."

They climbed the stairs to Griffin's bedroom.

"Want to play video games?" Griffin offered. "I have a sick collection."

He definitely did. It was another thing that Eric's mom was uptight about. Griffin had games that Eric wouldn't be allowed to play in a million years.

"This one is about an assassin from another galaxy," Griffin said, holding up the box. "It's pretty wicked. He's got mad skills. Lots of splurting blood, gushing up like geysers, it's hysterical."

"Do *you* want to play?" Eric cautiously asked.

Griffin threw the disk aside. "Nah, not really." He looked around the room, gestured to a cage on his desk. "We could torture my gerbil?"

For a minute—a second, really, maybe less than that—Eric thought Griffin might be serious. They locked eyes and there was something there, a passing darkness, then it was gone, like a storm cloud drifting away. Griffin smiled, laughed out loud. He was only joking.

He reached for a dark wooden box, about the size of a thick dictionary. "Want to see a few of my souvenirs?"

Griffin asked it with obvious pride. But Eric had to hide his disappointment when he looked through the contents. It was a weird assortment of random stuff, some kind of baseball pin, old coins, a pocketknife, a tooth, a couple of keys, a mishmash of junk.

"There's a story behind every one of those pieces," Griffin said.

"Oh yeah?" Eric pointed to the tooth. "What's the story with that?"

Griffin studied Eric's face. He took the box,

snapped it shut, and returned it to the shelf. "Maybe another time," he said.

"Sure, whatever," Eric answered, not knowing what else to say.

They talked for a while. A long time had passed since Eric had a normal conversation with someone his own age. Griffin wanted to know all about Eric—he asked tons of questions, very curious—and Eric, to his surprise, answered all of them.

"So," Griffin said. "Your dad isn't around at all?"

Eric touched on the major parts of the tale, leaving out a few key details. He told Griffin how his father took off one day, a spontaneous decision that was a long time coming. "It was like getting hit by a train," Eric told Griff. "You can see it coming from miles down the track. You try to get ready for it. But when it hits you, *wham*, you're still all messed up."

Eric added, "I guess my mom got tired of waiting for him to get his act together. So we moved here."

There was something about Griffin, the way he listened. Eric told Griffin things that he hadn't said to anyone, ever. For his part, Griffin was really nice about everything—he seemed to *understand*—like he'd already been there. Like he could see inside Eric, and knew how he felt, even when Eric himself wasn't so sure.

Griffin blew the hair out of his eyes. "I guess it sucks to be you."

"Some days, yeah, it does."

When it was time for Eric to go, the boys agreed to get together again, soon. Eric left the house with a sense of relief, like he'd just dropped off a heavy backpack. He kept so many things buried inside, it was good to finally say them out loud. Eric felt lighter.

Sure, Griffin was a different kind of guy, there was no question about that. He had his rough edges. He wasn't like Eric's old friends back in Ohio. But for one day, during those few hours, Griffin was what Eric needed.

He was, Eric believed, a friend.

11
[crazy]

ERIC PULLED THE ACOUSTIC GUITAR CLOSE TO HIS BELLY, leaned back on his bed, and strummed. He wasn't practicing anything in particular, just running through some songs. It was his way of checking out. He closed the bedroom door, disappeared into himself, and tried not to think. The guitar was his shield, the hard outer shell he needed, like the exoskeleton of some soft-bellied bug.

Whenever Eric thought about his father, when he remembered things, it left him confused. He didn't want to remember, didn't want to feel this way, but the memories flooded in like a rising river, ruining everything. There they were. He could picture it.

Rudy just a baby, probably asleep. It was dark out, his parents at the kitchen table, Eric spooning a bowl of vanilla ice cream, and his father's voice, loud and accusing.

"Clear the table?" his father screamed. "I'll clear the table, just watch me. I can be really helpful around the house." He picked up plates and glasses and tossed them one by one in underhanded arcs toward the sink. There they crashed and shattered—his mother crying, pleading for Eric's father to stop, please stop, please— but the clatter continued until, finally, the dishes cleared and a life splintered, his father walked out the door.

Oh, the way his mother sagged to the floor. Eric could see it in his mind, as if a motion picture were projected against the inner walls of his skull. She leaned against the wall and her legs slid forward. She dropped down, slumped over, face splotchy with tears. Eric didn't dare to move. He sat watching her while a thousand small fish swam through his bloodstream. Then he finally climbed down to the floor and crawled to her and whispered, "It's okay, Mom, it's okay, stop crying. I'll clean everything up."

"He's sick," she murmured in answer, staring at nothing. "He's so sick."

And rather than clean anything up, Eric bent his head to her warm soft lap and crashed. Just fell asleep right then and there, instantly.

No, Eric hadn't told Griffin that story. Some stories you don't tell. You just keep them to yourself, locked away, and you run the guitar pick up and down across six strings and you strum.

Eric couldn't tell Griffin the whole truth about his father. So it was a day of white lies—first to his mother, then to Griffin Connelly. It wasn't like Eric *wanted* to lie, exactly. It was just that the truth was so . . . inconvenient. To Eric's way of thinking, a good fiction was better than a hard fact. Everybody breathed easier; nobody got hurt; and you moved on to the next thing.

Even if he wanted to, how could Eric tell Griffin about what really happened back in Ohio? The truth was a slippery bar of soap, something ungraspable, a thing Eric himself could never understand, much less *tell*.

How do you say that your father has a "mental illness"? How do you say "schizophrenia" and not open a can of fresh wounds and questions? Schizophrenia was like a word from a bad horror movie, Dr. Jekyll and Mr. Dad. But it didn't work like that. His father didn't act like two people, a good guy and a bad guy. It was trickier than that. His father was once the greatest guy in the world, but then, slowly, over time, he wasn't anymore. He changed, got angry and confused. His own thoughts haunting him, hunting him down. His father fell into dark moods, made unfounded accusations, said crazy things. And worse: He dropped into long brooding silences, not speaking for days, a ghost walking around in Daddy's shoes. It was like he slowly vanished in front of Eric's eyes, from the inside out. A hollow man. A sunken-eyed scarecrow. In that way, his father *was* like two men, the good guy and the sick one. For Eric to ever live a full life, he knew that he would have to love both men. The well and the ill. He couldn't pick one or the other. It had to be both, for they were two sides of one man, his father.

How do you tell that story?

How do you describe the years of living with that? The best thing—the thing that worked for a while, anyway—was to pretend it wasn't happening. Repeat: *Dad's just fine.* Keep saying it, over and over, as if saying it enough might make it true. Eric was just a boy when things began to turn bad, soon after Rudy was born. On and off, in fits and spurts, the illness took hold, gripped his father like a snake in its coils and squeezed. But nobody talked about it for a long time, each trying to *not* know, figuring that if they ignored it, maybe it would go away. Maybe Eric's real father would reappear one morning, bright and chipper, "How ya doing, sport?" Except it never happened. Things only got worse. Until finally, they had to talk about it, Eric and his mom, had to say the words nobody wanted to hear.

"Your father is sick. He's been sick for a long time."

Sick? "Sick" was a cold, an upset stomach, a fever you recovered from. This wasn't the body being sick, it was the brain being sick. This was, in his mother's words, "mental illness."

There were doctors, yes, and stays at hospitals, an

ever-changing cocktail of little pills. The drugs helped in some ways, offered him some relief, but Eric could see the change in his father. The drugs drained him dry. His neck swelled up, his face twitched, he lost his spark. Eric's father complained about aches and sore parts. He once rubbed his chest and looked at Eric in wide-eyed alarm—"There's nothing there, there's nothing there"—rubbing his chest over and over, there where the heartbeat should be. "I can't *feel* anything," he'd cried.

But mostly, his father's essence had changed until it was as if his father on medication had no personality left. That was why, his mother explained, Eric's father stopped taking the doctor's pills. "He felt like he was losing himself, slipping away," she tried to explain. And it was true. Eric could see that it was true. On medicine, his father didn't act crazy anymore, but in some ways it was worse. A part of him had died. The part Eric loved.

His mother told Eric other things:

"He still loves you, he'll always love you."

"He's suffering right now. He's confused. He's overwhelmed. There are voices in his head."

She cried. She didn't want to cry in front of Eric, he could see that, his mother trying to be strong, but she couldn't be, not all the time. That was the other hard part. He couldn't lose her, too. And now there was Rudy to worry about.

It was scary. Because his father was still around, drifting aimlessly from room to room. When things were okay, when Eric didn't think about it too much, he could sit quietly in the same room with his father and feel . . . *good.* Pretend everything was okay. He still had a dad. Not just any dad, but *his* dad, his one and only. That guy over there, the innocent one with the gentle soul, who loved trees and music and laughter and his two sons, that swell guy whose thoughts were eating him alive.

Then some things happened—other memories now, the water of remembering rising ever higher—when Eric's father lost control, smashed a mirror and some lamps, ripped down the blinds off a bay window—and was gone the next morning before Eric awoke. And here was the truly shameful thing, the horror in Eric's heart: He was glad. Good riddance. Who needs to live with that?

People can lose a leg. People can get their hands stuck in machines and have their fingers torn off. Terrible car accidents robbed people of their sight, their ability to walk, their dreams and hopes of a healthy future. But there was nothing worse—nothing on this earth, of that Eric was sure—than losing your mind, your *peace* of mind, because that was like losing your self. It was losing everything.

His father was a walking absence, a faint duplicate, a watered-down version of his former self, without substance enough to cast a shadow.

There was no way Eric could tell Griffin Connelly that story. So he told bits and pieces and white lies. Eric wondered if Griffin sensed it, the whole truth, if somehow Griffin already *knew*, saw into Eric's secret heart and smiled.

12
[shiner]

AS SEPTEMBER GAVE WAY TO OCTOBER, ERIC BEGAN TO feel more at home in his new surroundings. His classes weren't too bad, and his teachers were fine. Sure, science with Mrs. Wilcox was deadly—she talked and talked—but there was nothing unusual about that. Eric supposed there were boring teachers no matter where you lived. It couldn't all be PE and recess.

He sometimes hung with Mary during home base. They weren't big friends or anything, but Eric felt like it was the beginning of something, though he had no idea what. Maybe he just liked her looks, her unfussy natural beauty. The weird kid, Hallenback, still stared darkly at Eric from time to time. *If looks could kill*, Eric thought. But for the most part, home base was about getting homework out of the way so that it didn't interfere with crucial television viewing.

If Eric had not yet been invited into Griffin Connelly's inner circle, he definitely had a seat at the lunch table. And for now, that's all Eric really desired. He was even beginning to like some of the other guys, Pat and Hakeem, in particular. Even Drew P. could be okay sometimes, when he ditched the tough-guy act and tried being himself.

Griffin was the group leader, the alpha dog. Depending upon his mood, he could be friendly and funny or dark and distant. Eric couldn't figure Griffin out. But even so, Eric found himself drawn to Griffin, the way a caveman might be attracted to fire. *The light, the heat, the danger.*

Along the wall where the line forms for students to buy hot lunch, there was a big GOT MILK? poster, featuring an enormous photo of a pop singer's smiling face: big sweep of blond hair, flawless skin (thanks, no doubt, to Photoshop), and milky mustache above a pearly white smile. Her head on the poster was gigantic, about three feet tall, or the height of a preschooler. Drew P. pulled a wad of gum from his mouth and stuck it on the singing starlet's left nostril. With a deft motion, he molded the gum into the shape of a drip. Drew P. stepped back and grinned, an artist satisfied with his creation.

"S'not bad, Droop," Cody commented.

"Truly disgusting," Eric agreed.

Just then Griffin brushed past the boys, head down and moving quickly, not turning to say hello, not even bothering to make fun of Cody's grease-stained jeans.

"What's up with Griff?" Eric asked.

"He's got a shiner," Drew P. said in a low voice.

"A what?"

"A black eye."

"He got into a fight?" Eric asked.

Drew P. checked to make sure that Griffin was seated at the table across the room. He whispered, "More like he got smacked around."

"Who did it?"

Cody interrupted, "What are you, writing a blog?"

"Just curious," Eric replied.

"Just curious," Cody repeated in a mocking tone.

Eric glared at Cody. That kid could be so annoying. But at the same time, he could see that Cody was being protective of Griffin. He was as loyal as a Doberman. "Tell me what happened," Eric said to Drew.

"You never met his dad, have you?"

Eric had not. He'd seen Griffin's father only once, about a week ago. He was sitting at the Connellys' kitchen table in a bathrobe, slump-shouldered, staring at a cereal box. Griffin didn't bother to introduce them, and Mr. Connelly never looked up.

"Retired city cop, not all that friendly," Drew P. explained. "Has to be—what?—at least six-four, two hundred seventy-five pounds."

"Scary dude," Cody murmured.

They moved through the line. Eric threw a square slice of pizza on his tray. Cody stuffed a buttered roll inside his shirt.

"The main problem is he's a drinker," Drew continued.

"Griff's father gave him that black eye?" Eric asked.

"Wow, Sherlock, you are a regular genius." Cody whistled. He picked up his tray and cut in front of

Eric. "Don't say anything to him, keep it on the down low. Shut up and mind your business."

Eric sat down diagonally across from Griffin and tried not to look. It was impossible. Griffin's eye looked worse from up close, swollen with ugly shades of blue and purple. Griffin kept his head down, hair dangling over his eyes, and ate in silence. After a few minutes, Griffin glanced up and caught Eric staring at him. He locked eyes with Eric, daring him to look away.

Then the strangest thing happened. Almost in slow motion, Griffin pushed his hair back and turned his head to give Eric a better look, the way a model might pose for a photographer. Griffin's long, slender fingers went to his eye, tips lightly touching the tender, bruised skin, a blind boy reading Braille. *What did it say? What story did it tell?*

Griffin did not show any expression. There was no emotion there. His face was battered and blank. His eyes, cold.

Eric shivered, and looked away.

13
[pretzel]

GRIFFIN'S MOOD DARKENED OVER THE COURSE OF LUNCH, and he stalked outside for recess, hands buried in his pockets.

"Hey, guys. Hi, Griff!"

The voice—too loud, too high-pitched—could mean only one person, David Hallenback. The kid who could not, or would not, take a hint.

Hallenback often appeared on the fringes of the group, like a mosquito hovering around a campfire, close but careful not to get burned. He was the butt of jokes, the fool, the kid with the KICK ME sign taped to his back. No one seemed to like him, but by virtue of pure persistence, Hallenback was tolerated. His presence offered a form of entertainment value, comic relief from the routine of endless school days. He was the fly that got swatted, the spider without legs, and in that sense the boys didn't really mind Hallenback's uninvited appearances.

Usually.

"Not today, Hallenback," Cody said. "Go away."

Unfazed, Hallenback peered at Griffin. "What happened to your eye, Griff? Huh?"

"Hallenback, Jesus Christ," Cody hissed. "Go. Away."

This type of scene had lately become a frequent occurrence. It was as if David Hallenback suffered from amnesia. No matter what happened, he kept coming back for more, desperate for acceptance. The truth was he had nowhere else to go. So no matter how hard he got shoved away, Hallenback always seemed to dust himself off and bounce back. It was a disastrous strategy for making friends. The tension was increasing, but Hallenback couldn't—or wouldn't—grasp it.

It started the way it usually did. The boys made a

few one-liners at Hallenback's expense. Some name-calling. Nasty stuff. Hallenback just sort of nodded and chortled, absorbing the insults, his soft belly quavering under his shirt.

"I didn't see you on the bus today, Hallenback," Cody said. "Oh, that's right. Your mommy picks you up these days, doesn't she? Isn't that special."

"Not always," Hallenback answered. "I walk sometimes."

"We miss you on the bus, Hallenback," Drew P. complained. "We don't have anywhere to shoot our spitballs. We're getting rusty."

The boys glanced to Griffin for approval. It was as if, Eric realized, this was all a performance for Griffin's benefit. He was the ultimate audience—every move, every word intended for his eyes and ears.

The group was gathered in a vibrant, pulsing, huddled mass. From where they stood, several noon aides had a good view of them.

Hallenback gamely laughed along as the name-calling continued. He smiled as if he were in on the joke. But slowly you could see his eyes narrow and the corners of his mouth turn down. He was rattled, and they could see it.

Just walk away, Hallenback, Eric thought.

But Hallenback stood there, still looking to Griffin for help, for some sign of assistance. He had no idea how to tell them to quit it. Finally, in a high-pitched, sing-songy voice, Hallenback crowed: "Sticks and stones may break my bones, but names will never hurt me."

Yes, he actually said it.

And no, it didn't help.

Cody laughed. "Maybe I should get some sticks and stones, huh, what do you think, Hallenback? That a good idea? Should I pick up a rock?"

"Get lost, Hallenback," Drew P. urged. He roughly spun Hallenback around, gave him a push. "We don't want you here."

"Hey, leave him alone!"

They turned to stare at Griffin, who had said it. He raised his chin, gestured toward the building. Two noon aides stood together, their eyes upon them.

"Come on, David," Griffin called to Hallenback. "Let's take a walk over to the big tree."

Hallenback hesitated. He looked back to the building. The tree was in the opposite direction, out of the line of sight. "I don't know—"

"You want to hang out, don't you?" Griffin asked. He smiled, put an arm around Hallenback's shoulder. "We're all going to hang out by the tree. You are welcome to come . . . or not. It's up to you."

And at that, Griffin started walking to the tree. He didn't once look back to see if anybody else was coming. Because he already knew. They'd all follow. Cody, Will, Drew, Eric. Every single one of them.

Even Hallenback.

"The name of this game," Griffin announced once they arrived at the big oak, "is called Pretzel. Have you ever played it, David?"

Hallenback brought a hand to the back of his neck and rubbed it. He appeared doubtful. He shook his head once, no.

"There's nothing wrong with that," Griffin answered. He was upbeat now, energized, happy. "It's like wrestling. Here, let me show you."

The rest of the boys gathered in a sort of ring,

forming a barricade that sealed Hallenback off from the school building. The noon aides wouldn't be able to see much.

In a swift motion, Griffin gripped Hallenback's wrist and yanked hard. Hallenback fumbled into Griffin, who shouldered him in the chest. *Wham.* The blow stunned him. Hallenback's head snapped back.

Griffin stepped with his left leg and planted it behind the slow-moving Hallenback. With a compact shove, Griffin pushed Hallenback to the ground, where he landed hard on his upper back.

"Hey, get up, man!" Griffin chuckled, hauling the bewildered boy up by his shirt. Griffin roughly slapped the dirt off Hallenback. All smiles and laughter.

"Good times," Cody murmured, licking his lips. "Good times."

Now Griffin applied pressure on Hallenback's wrist, twisting it, bending the arm around his back.

"So," Griffin said, lecturing to the group. "Can anyone in class please tell me why this game is called Pretzel?"

Cody's hand shot into the air. "I know! I know!"

Hallenback was on his tiptoes now, an anxious look swimming in his eyes. The back of his shirt was dirt-stained. He groaned softly. "I—uh—"

"Did you say something, David?" Griffin asked. With another move, he had the boy in a new painful entanglement. "This is called the chicken wing. Isn't that a funny name, David?"

"Ow, that hurts—"

"What? Are you talking to me?"

"My arm—you're hurting me."

Eric could hear the new urgency in Hallenback's voice. And something else in it, too: a growing terror. Yet Eric did not move, did not raise a hand to help.

"Griff!" a voice suddenly warned. "Diaz is coming."

In an instant, Griffin pushed Hallenback into the group, turned, and locked arms with Drew P. in an animated wrestling match. The rest of the boys laughed and let out whoops of encouragement, cheering the spectacle of their phony match.

"What's going on here?" asked Mrs. Diaz.

"The Ultimate Fighting Championships!" Cody

replied. "It was on TV last night. Hallenback"—he paused, corrected himself—"I mean, David and some of the guys were showing us."

"You know the playground rules," Mrs. Diaz stated. She wasn't buying a word of it and could scarcely conceal her distaste for Cody.

"We're sorry, Mrs. Diaz," Griffin said, stepping forward. "We were fooling around and maybe got too rough."

"Boys will be boys," Drew P. clucked.

The noon aide nodded doubtfully. She scanned the group. "David?" she asked. "Are you all right?"

All eyes turned to David Hallenback. He held his right elbow in his left hand, cradled close to his body. The boy looked like a wounded, moist baby bird. "Just playing," he said, looking at the grass, "goofing around." Tears welled in his eyes; he bravely tried to blink them away.

The recess bell sounded, three times.

"Oh man, I can't be late for Mr. Foy—he's giving a test today," Will said. The gang of boys headed back to the building.

Eric found himself walking beside Griffin.

"Look back," Griffin whispered. "What do you see?"

Eric glanced back at the great old oak. Mrs. Diaz was talking with David, heads close together. She touched his arm; he pulled it away.

Eric shook his head. "That was kind of rough, don't you think?"

"Hallenback's fine," Griffin snapped. "Besides, he won't say much. He knows better than that."

Eric measured his words carefully. "It just seemed . . . unnecessary."

"Really? Is that what you think, Eric?" Griffin said, his voice drenched with sarcasm. "Because I didn't do anything wrong. What about you? Ever wonder: *What did I do?* Because all I remember is you standing there with a big smile on your face."

"I wasn't smiling—"

Griffin dismissed him with a wave of his hand. "Shut up, Eric. Or maybe next time it will be you."

14
[flinch]

OVER THE REST OF THE WEEK, ERIC WITNESSED A NUMBER
of incidents that involved David Hallenback. Mostly
stupid stuff, nothing that seemed all that bad, like
somebody reaching out to flick David's ears as they
passed in the hallway, or another guy stepping on the
back of his sneaker, giving David a flat tire. Maybe it
had been going on since the beginning of September—
or maybe even for years—and Eric hadn't really noticed.
But now when he walked down the hall, Eric's eyes
were open. He saw that David Hallenback—that weird,

awkward, mush-faced kid—was having a pretty rough time.

I Dare You! seemed to be the hot new game that October. The rules were simple: You dared someone to do something really stupid and you laughed when they did it. Laughed at them, or with them, it didn't matter, just so long as there was laughter.

For that, Hallenback was the perfect pawn, seemingly willing to do anything for approval—no matter how humiliating, or cruel, or pathetic. That was the carrot Griffin so expertly dangled: acceptance.

The dares were anything that would provide momentary entertainment for the bored boys of Bellport Central Middle School:

Go into the nurse's office, barking like a seal.

Wear your pants backwards all day.

Put a tack on Betsy Hurley's chair.

Steal a milk carton when Mr. Hennessey wasn't looking.

I dare you, I double-dare you.

The Flinch was another schooltime classic. It always got a laugh, and it worked like this. Hallenback or any other likely suspect—it didn't absolutely have to

be Hallenback; he was just the Flavor of the Month—
might be at his locker, whiffing on his asthma inhaler.
Drew P. would stride up to him, make a fist, and rear
back like he was about to deliver a punch. Seeing this,
Hallenback would shrink back in fear at the impending
blow. Many found it *hysterical.* Cody would laugh and
laugh at the look on Hallenback's face, his blubbering
gob of a mouth. *What a loser.*

Sometimes he squealed, "Ow!"—without even getting punched.

"Gotcha!" Drew would chortle.

Good times, good times.

Through it all, Eric didn't say a word. He was innocent, Eric reminded himself, he never participated
in the pranks. He never lifted a finger to harm David
Hallenback. He didn't think it was funny, so he usually walked away, pretending not to see. But Eric did
see. Just like all the other kids in the halls. And he
slowly began to recognize it for what it was.

*Terrorism in jeans. It comes with a laugh and a
loose-leaf binder.*

One day, while walking down a near-empty hallway, Eric turned a corner and there he was, David

Hallenback. Eric instinctively lifted his hand in greeting, a private hello that nobody else had to see.

And Hallenback *flinched*.

He pulled back when he saw Eric's hand come up.

Eric saw a glint in Hallenback's eye, a flash of fear. Eric sidestepped quickly, palms out—*hey, easy*—showing he intended no harm.

Hallenback stared at the tops of his shoes and scurried down the hall, like a rat looking for a hole.

I'm just as bad as the rest of them, Eric realized.

A picture replayed in Eric's mind. A memory. He sat at a round table, spooning vanilla ice cream into his mouth. His father tossed dishes into the sink, exploding like grenades. His mother cried, frantic, desperate. And Eric remembered the taste in his mouth, so cold and so sweet.

He found a fountain and took a long, deep drink. Things would have to change.

15
[visitor]

"ERIC!" HIS MOTHER CALLED UP THE STAIRS. "YOU HAVE a visitor."

He found Griffin Connelly waiting at the front door.

"Oh, hi."

"Is it okay?" Griffin asked. "I was just wondering if, maybe, we could hang out a little?"

"No, no—I mean, sure—no problem," Eric sputtered. "Come on in. I was just, um—"

"I know I shouldn't just invite myself over."

Eric didn't answer at first. It was a surprise to see Griffin standing in the living room. His black eye was barely noticeable anymore. The boys hadn't talked much since that trouble at recess. "It's good to see you," he said, and almost meant it.

Griffin nodded, head bobbing and weaving, like a boxer ducking punches. "You haven't been around much."

"Yeah, like, sooo busy. Tons of homework and, like, I've been doing some dog walking for the neighbors and—"

"Dog walking, huh?"

"It's not as glamorous as it sounds," Eric joked.

Griffin laughed. "Good money though, right?"

"It's okay."

There was a moment of silence, with the two boys standing in opposition.

Griffin scratched his nose with the back of his thumb. "So."

Eric called to the kitchen, "Mom? We're going to go up in my room, okay?"

Since Mrs. Hayes first met Griffin at the supermarket, she had seen him only a couple of other times, and always in her house. Whenever Griffin had invited

Eric over, Mrs. Hayes had come up with a reason why not: too much homework, they needed to go shopping, chores to be done, whatever. She said she liked Eric home, but he suspected there was more to it than that. Mrs. Hayes didn't say it outright, but it seemed to Eric that perhaps his mother's initial enthusiasm for Griffin Connelly had cooled to something else. It was not like her to answer the door and hastily retreat to the kitchen.

Eric had a futon in his room that doubled as a spare bed. Griffin sank into it, while Eric sat on the floor, leaning back on his hands.

Griffin smiled, but it didn't quite reach his eyes. He rubbed his hands on his jeans. "Where's Rudy?"

"He's been adopted by the family down the block," Eric quipped. "They've got twins and Rudy fits right in. He's like the triplet they never had."

Griffin crossed his arms, looked around the room. It was like he had something to say, but no idea how to say it. For the first time since Eric had known him, Griffin seemed unsure of himself.

"So," Eric said, stealing Griffin's line. "What's up?"

Griffin snorted, looked away. "Are you mad at me? It feels like things got weird between us after Hallenback got hurt at recess."

"He didn't *get* hurt," Eric insisted. "You hurt him. There's a difference."

Griffin's eyes rounded. "We were just fooling around."

Eric frowned, unsatisfied. "Look, I don't know what there is to talk about."

"I don't know why I did it," Griffin suddenly blurted.

He looked Eric in the eye. And Eric knew it was as true as anything Griffin had ever said to him. Griffin didn't know why.

"I just . . ." Griffin raised his hands in two fists, let them drop. "Everybody keeps asking me the same question. The principal, the house leader, Mrs. Ryan, or that stupid counselor, Mr. Floyd: *Why did you do it?* Why, why, why?" He said in a firm voice, "And I'm telling you, I don't know. I just did it."

Eric's shoulders flickered, the slightest of shrugs.

"You know that tooth you once asked me about?" Griffin began.

"Tooth? Oh, the one in that wooden box in your room? Yeah, I remember."

"Do you still want to know?"

"Sure, yeah, whatever." Eric feigned indifference.

A whisper of a smile came to Griffin's face. Once again, he was back in control. "It was my tooth." He opened his mouth wide, pointing. "That's a cap, see? My real tooth got knocked out in a fight."

Eric wondered why Griffin was telling him this story. Had he come over to say exactly this? "What's the point?" Eric asked.

"The point?" Griffin shook his head. "We're the same, that's the point."

The same? Eric didn't speak. A storm seemed to pass inside his brain, full of clouds and rain, and it was hard to hold on to one clear thought, just those words: *the same, the same.* He seemed to feel everything at once: denial, disgust, and the fear that Griffin Connelly might be right.

Grinning, Griffin tapped a fingernail against a tooth. *Click, click.* "That's right," he said. "Courtesy of dear old Dad. He's a mean drunk."

Eric thought about Griffin's black eye. About

Griffin's father in a ragged bathrobe, slumped in a kitchen chair, slurping down a bowl of cereal. The breakfast of champions. Eric thought about the way Hallenback could be such an annoying pest. Maybe there were good reasons why things happened the way they did. And maybe none of it mattered anyway. Griffin Connelly was a bully. That was the stone-cold fact. In the end, did it matter why?

"All those people say they want to help me," Griffin sneered. "You should sit in a room with them sometime, Eric. It's all smiles and politeness and concerned expressions. They tell me how they know I'm really a good kid deep down."

The contempt in Griffin's voice was thick. "They don't know me. I can see right through them. Bunch of liars."

Eric didn't know what to say. "I'm going to get some chips or something," he said, rising and moving to the door.

"Just no pretzels," Griffin joked.

"Right," Eric said, remembering Hallenback. "Maybe we should stay away from pretzels for a while."

When Eric got back to the room, Griffin wasn't there. But he entered a minute later. "Bathroom," he explained.

His mood seemed different. Lighter, somehow. "You know, it's not like I did anything *that* bad," he told Eric. "Let's face it. Kids like Hallenback are always going to get beat on. It's the law of the jungle. Only the strong survive."

"We're in middle school," Eric countered. "Not a jungle."

Griffin shook his head. Just like that, the old confidence was back. "No, you're wrong. It's still a jungle, the survival of the fittest. The sooner you figure that out, Eric, the better."

"I don't believe that," Eric said.

Griffin blinked, blew the bangs out of his eyes. They had hit an impasse. "When you think about it, Eric, we're all basically animals. I think that's why I was fed up with Hallenback that day. I mean, come on, you've seen those nature shows on television. Hallenback is like the sick gazelle in the herd, limping along. The one that gets eaten. It's not fair, but that's life. I don't make the rules."

Eric listened, didn't answer.

"You, of all people, know I'm right," Griffin persisted. "Don't try to con me. You know what it's like. We're all animals. That's why you called Cody a weasel."

"It was a stupid thing to say," Eric countered. "I didn't mean it."

Griffin grinned. "Sure." He stood and slowly wandered around the room, running a finger along the spines of books on the shelves, bending to read the plaques on Eric's Little League trophies. Griffin picked up a small pile of CD-Rs, the songs and artists written out by a careful hand.

Eric reached for them, a little too hastily.

Griffin pulled away, sensing their value. He read one out loud: " 'Eric, Rock On! Love, Dad.' Aw, isn't that sweet!" he teased.

"Give me those," Eric demanded.

Griffin spun around, pretending to tuck them into his shirt. When Eric grabbed his arm, Griffin laughed. "Here you go—chill out, buddy. I'm just messing with you."

"It's not funny."

"Don't get all sensitive on me, Eric." Griffin could see that Eric was flustered. He seemed to take pleasure in it.

Eric glanced at the digital clock, the way a drowning man might scan the water in hope of a life preserver. "Look, it's getting—"

"Yeah, yeah, I've got to go anyway."

Eric escorted Griffin down the stairs and out the door. He watched Griffin pick up a skateboard and push off down the driveway and into the street. No helmet, naturally. Eric felt relieved—and more confused than ever.

What is he up to? Eric wondered.

Later that night, after dinner, Rudy made a discovery. Teary-eyed, he came into the television room holding his ceramic baseball bank. "I'm missing twenty-seven dollars. All my birthday money is gone."

Two sets of eyes—Rudy's and his mother's—settled on Eric. "Don't look at me. I never touched your money."

Rudy's lip quivered. "Mom?"

"Are you sure, Rudy? Maybe you misplaced it."

Rudy was positive. "But if Eric didn't take it, and Mom, if you didn't take it . . ."

Mrs. Hayes fixed her eyes on Eric. The look on her face said it all. She had a pretty good idea where the money had gone.

A sudden thought leaped into Eric's mind. A few minutes later, he went to check on his CDs.

The gifts from his father.

One of them was missing.

16
[mary]

GINGER, A LONG-HAIRED GOLDEN RETRIEVER, WAS READY to bound out the door when Eric arrived to take her for a Saturday-afternoon walk. The minute she heard the keys rattle outside the door—Eric always struggled with the Martins' sticky deadbolt—Ginger would leap out of her socks. If, of course, she were wearing any (she wasn't).

The dog-walking business had turned out well for Eric. Back in Ohio, he once took care of a neighbor's dog when they went away on vacation. That job led to others, and Eric considered it easy money. He just had to be trustworthy and responsible, and those qualities came naturally enough. Now on Long Island, Eric had two steady clients, the Parkers and the Oropesas, plus some side jobs when people went away for weekend trips or vacations. He didn't have to do much to drum up business, just hung up a poster at the coffee shop in town. He'd walk the dogs in the morning and evening, play with them a little, give them food, water, and something resembling love, and that was it. Besides, Eric liked dogs. They were a lot simpler than human beings.

On a walk with Ginger the day after Griffin's visit, Eric came across Mary in front of a large, brown house. She was raking a pile of leaves down to the curbside.

Eric lingered there, letting Ginger sniff around, hoping that Mary would notice him. "Hey." She finally smiled.

In truth, she seemed more interested in Ginger than in Eric, but he could live with that, happily. Mary bent down to greet the perky golden, who strained on the leash, lapping up the attention. Thoroughly slimed by sloppy kisses, Mary enthused, "I didn't know you had a dog."

"She's not mine," Eric replied. He told her about his dog-walking business. "You live here?"

"No, I just randomly rake leaves at strangers' houses," she deadpanned.

"Oh. Dumb question, I guess."

She smiled at Eric, then spoke directly to Ginger in a high-pitched trill that, Eric figured, she reserved exclusively for canines: "You look thirsty. Are you thirsty, with your long tongue hanging out? I'll get you some water, that's right, you wait one minute. I'll be right back."

Ginger seemed to think this was a great idea. Eric was okay with it, too.

While Ginger slurped from a Tupperware bowl, Eric relaxed the leash and sat on the curb alongside Mary. He thought about Griffin, and David Hallenback, and what had happened yesterday with Rudy's money. Eric wanted to talk about it, but he wasn't sure if he could trust Mary. *Was she one of them?* So he danced around the subject. "What have you been up to? I haven't seen you hanging out with Griffin and Cody and those guys," he said.

Mary intently tore at a maple leaf, until only the

skeletal veins remained. "I'm trying to stay away from them," she confessed. "Too much weirdness."

"Oh?"

Mary shrugged, picked up another leaf, and began the shredding process over again.

"Griffin can be . . ." Eric paused, trying to find the right words, "I don't know, kind of hard to figure out."

Mary snorted. "It takes a while, but you'll figure him out eventually."

"Do you want to give me any tips?"

Mary smiled tightly, her lips stretched thin. "I don't want to talk about him, to tell you the truth."

"Okay, sure." Eric looked away, stood up.

"Do you want company?" Mary asked.

"Really?"

"Beats raking."

"Yeah, that'd be great."

"There's a dog park not far from here," Mary suggested. "Ginger can run around off-leash."

It was Eric's first time alone with Mary. Of course, not counting Ginger's company. The dog somehow made it easier, gave them a third thing, something outside of themselves that they could share. Mary found an old tennis ball, hurled it across the field. Ginger took off like a rocket, proudly retrieving it. Just an animal, doing what came naturally. They played that game for a long while, Eric and Mary taking turns throwing the ball, Ginger tireless and impatient.

A few times Mary's cell phone sounded. She'd flip it open, read a text message, flip it closed.

At a certain point she stopped talking.

"You're frowning," Eric noted. "Is something the matter?"

Mary shook her head. But a moment later she pulled out her cell, punched a few buttons, and handed it to Eric. "Here, look at this."

There was a photograph of a girl's thick body. She wore shorts and a midriff-baring shirt, with the head of a pig Photoshopped onto it. "Who's this supposed to be?" Eric asked.

"That's Chantel Williams, you know her?"

"Sort of, we're in a couple of classes together."

"Well, everybody is really mad at her—"

"Everybody?"

"Okay, not everybody," Mary replied, conceding

the point. "It's mostly Chrissie and Alexis. They want me to come over, because they want to get her back."

Eric didn't know Chantel well. She seemed okay. "What did she do?"

"Flirted with the wrong guy, according to Alexis." After a pause, Mary confessed, "I know, you don't have to say anything. It's all so stupid."

"What are they going to do?"

Ginger dropped the ball at Eric's feet, then plopped to the ground herself, exhausted. He picked the ball up and threw it. Ginger watched it sail through the air, but did not otherwise stir.

"Go on, go get it!" Eric urged.

Ginger rested her chin on the cool earth. She wasn't going anywhere. The ball could stay lost forever.

It was time to go. Eric reattached Ginger's leash and gave a tug. He reminded Mary that she still hadn't answered his question.

Mary sighed, shrugged, rearranged a loose strand of hair. "Something mean," she said, eyes narrowing. "They are talking about maybe some fake Web page. Alexis has a new iMac in her room. They want me to help. I'm good with computers."

"You've done stuff like that before?"

Mary looked away, nodded. "A little bit."

"So are you going over there?"

"No, I'm sick of it," Mary said with surprising conviction. "Girls are the worst. We can be so freaking mean."

Eric laughed. "Guys aren't always so great, either, you know."

"Yeah, but at least a guy will punch you in the face, you know what I mean? They do it and then it's over. But with girls, we slice you up piece by piece. It's like death by a thousand cuts."

Eric playfully pushed Ginger on the rump. He told the animal, "Good thing you're a dog, Ginger. Life is simple. Eat, walk, poop, let somebody else pick it up. You don't have to deal with any of this crap—not even your own."

They walked in silence for a while longer.

"Want to get a slice of pizza at Mario's?" Eric offered. "My treat."

They dropped Ginger off at the Martins' house. Mary came inside, but waited by the door while Eric went into the kitchen to give Ginger a fresh bowl of water. Eric picked up an envelope with his name on it; two twenty-dollar bills were inside. "They go away a lot," Eric explained. "But they, like, totally trust me. Really nice people." He locked the house and put the spare keys in his pocket.

"I feel sorry for Ginger," Mary said. "It must be boring for her alone in that big, fancy house."

Then Mary said something that Eric couldn't quite hear. "What?"

"Nothing," Mary answered. "I was thinking about Chantel. I guess I said, 'Poor Chantel.' "

Eric touched her on the shoulder, letting his hand rest there for a moment. "Well, at least you aren't a part of it."

"Yeah," Mary said. "I haven't done anything. I wonder why it feels like I did?"

17

[slander]

AROUND THAT TIME, ONE OF THE SCHOOL COUNSELORS, the loose-limbed, goateed Mr. Floyd, came into Eric's science class. The topic of the day was "Bullying: Rumors and Gossip."

Mr. Floyd explained that it was a normal thing they do a few times every year. He reminded the class that he'd given a similar talk in early September. Even so, Eric wondered if this particular visit might be in response to what had been swirling around the hallways for the past few weeks.

After setting some guidelines—everybody had to listen to and respect one another, basically—Mr. Floyd began by reminding the class of the definition of bullying. He read from the screen, "Bullying is whenever someone uses his or her power unfairly or repeatedly to hurt someone."

Eric glanced around the classroom. Pat Daly was in there, along with Hakeem, and Drew Peterson. A couple of Mary's friends, Chrissie and Alexis, were in the class, along with Mary herself; at times, Eric couldn't help but feel that Mr. Floyd was speaking directly to those girls.

Mr. Floyd said there were four types of bullying: verbal, physical, intimidation, and indirect bullying. Today, he seemed most interested in indirect bullying. When Mr. Floyd asked for examples, a bunch of students spoke up, mentioning things like lies and gossip. One by one, different students told about their experiences, either as targets or bullies or bystanders. Except they always said things like "I know a kid who knows a girl who . . ." or, "It didn't happen to me, but . . ."

Yeah, right, Eric thought.

Tamara Agee admitted, "I've teased people about the way they looked," she said. "I didn't think it was bullying."

Drew Peterson raised his hand. "Are you doing this in all the classes, or just ours?"

"I'll be presenting this to every student in grade seven," Mr. Floyd said. "No one is being singled out. But," he admitted, "there have been some things going on lately that we're not happy about."

Eric could almost *hear* Chrissie's eyeballs roll in their sockets. By her body language—long torso poured across her desk, head resting on her arm—Chrissie made it clear that she was *soooo* bored by everything.

Mr. Floyd steered the discussion to rumors and how they spread. He asked, "What is slander?"

Together the class decided that slander was like a mean rumor, done purposely to hurt someone. When he asked if anyone knew of any examples, about six hands instantly shot up. Some girls found mean notes in their lockers, or received anonymous phone calls, all sorts of brutal stuff. Eric was fascinated and horrified at the same time. Mostly, though, he felt relieved, once again, for the 937th time in his life, that he was born a boy. Those girls were murder on one another.

Through it all, Mary never moved. She sat perfectly still, eyes fixed forward. Once, she almost raised her hand to speak. Eric saw her lean forward, tighten her grip on the desk, but then she seemed to think better of it.

She never said a word.

The fun part was when they got to play classroom *Jeopardy!* Mr. Floyd had a big whiteboard, with four main categories: 1) How Can You Stop Bullies? 2) Rumors; 3) Types of Bullying; and 4) Grab Bag. Each category had five questions, ranging from one hundred to five hundred points.

When it was Eric's turn to pick, he landed on a Double Jeopardy question. Mr. Floyd read from a card, "A person who witnesses a bullying situation."

Eric sat in silence, uncomfortable in his own skin. So he waited, head down, pretending to think. A couple of boys hummed the *Jeopardy!* theme song, "Do-do-DO-do do-do-DO . . ."

"Buzz! Time's up," Mr. Floyd announced. "Anyone else have the answer?"

"What is . . . bystander?!" someone shouted.

"Correct! For eight hundred points!"

For the last few minutes, each group had to brainstorm a list of strategies to create a bully-free zone. The clock was ticking and Asi, the writer in Eric's group, had to scribble really fast:

- respect
- tell an adult
- don't spread rumors
- don't encourage a bully
- stand up for a friend
- walk away
- don't be a bystander
- help victims
- say "stop it!"
- don't laugh at bully's jokes
- be nice to target

Everybody had lots of ideas. It was fun. Besides, it beat listening to another dull lecture from his science teacher, Mrs. Wilcox. Anything was better than that. Eric's thoughts turned to Griffin Connelly, then David

Hallenback. Eric decided that he'd try a little harder. Like Mr. Floyd said, be an "ally," not a bystander.

All the while, Eric kept glancing over at Mary. She was staring out the window, picking at the frayed hems of her jeans.

18
[story]

ENGLISH WAS ERIC'S LAST CLASS, THE HAPPY PERIOD AT the end of the day's long sentence. But when Mr. Scofield heard a few boys joking about Mr. Floyd's presentation earlier in the day, he snapped, "You think it's funny?"

"Kind of, a little bit," one boy demurred. "It was fun, Mr. Scofield. We even played *Jeopardy!*"

"*Jeopardy!?* Jeopardy!? This isn't a game." Mr. Scofield snapped a piece of chalk in half. It echoed like a gunshot. "Put away that snack, Emily," he demanded. "Everyone, desks cleared. No talking. Eyes on me."

"Why are you being such a grouch, Mr. Scofield?" Emily asked. "We haven't done anything."

Mr. Scofield turned and strode to the chalkboard. He wrote hastily, the chalk clicking against the board: WE DO WHAT WE'RE TOLD.

He read the words in a slow, loud voice: "We do what we're told."

A few kids grumbled. Mr. Scofield replied sharply, "I am not *asking* for your cooperation—it's a requirement. Is that understood?"

His face reddened. The vein in his forehead flared. It was the first time Eric had seen Mr. Scofield so angry.

The class responded with silence.

Mr. Scofield wiped the chalk dust off his hands. He launched into a story. "In the early 1960s, a Yale professor named Stanley Milgram wondered about the Nazi atrocities in Germany. The Holocaust. The slaughter of six million Jews. How was it, Milgram wondered, that these German soldiers could have participated in such unspeakable acts? Someone had to light the ovens. Someone had to stand by and watch it happen. How could these ordinary men and women have allowed this to go on?

"So Milgram set up an experiment. He recruited forty volunteers. They were average, everyday people, like you or me."

Eric's eyes roamed around the room. A few kids had their heads on their desks, but overall, they seemed to be listening. Even Mary.

The volunteers, Scofield explained, were brought to a laboratory where they met a distinguished-looking scientist in a white lab coat. One by one, each volunteer met a man whom he or she believed to be a middle-aged accountant. After drawing the short straw, the accountant was selected to be the "learner" in the experiment. "The volunteers did not realize," the teacher said, "that the accountant was actually a professional actor, hired to play a role. The selection process was rigged."

A boy called out, "They were punked!"

Mr. Scofield nodded. "Yes, you could say that."

Each volunteer was assured that this was important research. They had critical jobs to perform. The accountant/actor was taken to an adjacent room, where he was hooked up with wires to a large electrical generator. The scientist in the lab coat then asked the man a series of questions. If he replied incorrectly, the volunteer was instructed to flip a switch, delivering an electric shock to the accountant.

"Here's where it gets interesting," Mr. Scofield said.

"Finally," Mary joked. The class laughed, but quickly grew quiet. They were already curious.

"The machine had thirty switches, all carefully labeled, ranging from fifteen volts all the way up to four hundred and fifty volts of electricity. With each shock," Mr. Scofield said, "the volunteer was told to increase the voltage. The switches were not actually connected to the electrical generator, but the volunteers did not realize that.

"As the experiment progressed, the accountant began to moan in pain, then scream, then frantically pound the walls. He begged and pleaded for them to stop the experiment. Hearing this, fourteen out of forty volunteers refused to continue. But twenty-six others ignored the cries and completed the experiment. They delivered all thirty shocks, all the way to the maximum level."

Mr. Scofield looked around the room. "I'm sure that some of those twenty-six people—like you and me—began to have doubts. They sensed it was wrong. They wanted to stop. But each time, the scientist told them in a firm voice that it was essential to continue the experiment. So they followed orders."

He pointed at the chalkboard: WE DO WHAT WE'RE TOLD.

"Do you understand?"

The class remained silent, thinking it through, not really getting it. Some watched the clock, began to gather books; the bell was about to sound.

"Think for yourself!" Mr. Scofield urged his students. His eyes seemed to linger on Mary. "It doesn't matter what other people do. You have to look into your own heart."

"What's this got to do with us?" a boy asked.

"Everything," the teacher answered. "It's about having the courage to do the right thing."

The bell rang. Eric grabbed his books and headed for the door. Mr. Scofield pointed to a photograph of Martin Luther King Jr. that had been tacked to the bulletin board. "King called it *'the appalling silence.'*"

Scofield was on his feet now, still teaching even after the bell, still declaiming quotes. "In the end we will remember not the words of our enemies, but the silence of our friends."

Strange guy, that Scofield. A little hyper sometimes.

But the image stuck in Eric's head like a dart to a wall: a man attached to wires, pounding on walls, pleading, "Stop, somebody please, make them stop." It was hard to pretend that the wires were not, in some strange inexplicable way, connected to him.

19
[reaching]

RUDY WAS PLAYING NERF BASKETBALL WHEN ERIC strolled into his bedroom. Rudy looked hopefully at his big brother. Nerf was way more fun with two people.

Eric went to the small bookshelf against the wall. He counted out twenty-seven dollars—a twenty, five, and two ones—and smoothed them on the shelf.

Rudy watched with astonishment.

"You took it?"

Eric didn't bother to deny it. "Just tell Mom you found it."

"But—"

"You got your money back, okay, it doesn't matter who took it," Eric snapped. "Tell Mom it was under your bed or something, I don't care, just don't say I paid you."

Rudy clawed at the back of his knee. He didn't say yes and he didn't say no. Then he offered up the ball. "Do you wanna—?"

"I don't," Eric said.

Eric closed the door, returned to his room, sprawled on the bed, his mood sour. After three minutes of staring at the ceiling, he came back to Rudy's door, apologized, said of course he'd love to play. "But," he promised, wagging a finger, "I will destroy you."

"Oh yeah!" Rudy exclaimed, rising to the challenge. He loved trash talk. Rudy fired a long shot from across the room—which Eric swatted away—and the game was on.

Eric had been undecided over how to handle Griffin Connelly. Should he risk confronting Griffin about the stolen money and the CD? Or should he just let it go? Eric didn't know how he'd react until the moment when he passed Griffin in the hall, coming from opposite directions. They saw each other and locked eyes, not speaking, not slowing. Then Eric felt his head tip; he gave Griffin a nod of recognition. Griffin nodded back. And it was over.

They had silently agreed to pretend nothing ever happened, or at least not to talk about it. The damage had already been done.

It wasn't about the money. It was about knowledge. Now Eric knew what Griffin was all about. Twenty-seven bucks and a CD was the price he had to pay. But now he *knew*. It was like a switch flipping on, a darkened room suddenly filling with light.

The truly puzzling thing was, it was as if Griffin *wanted* Eric to know. It was almost why he came over in the first place. Griffin had removed the mask; the wolf stepped out from beneath sheep's clothing and revealed himself, gnashing his teeth, showing his claws. There could be no more doubt. But at the same time, he made a point of telling Eric that story about how his father knocked out Griffin's tooth. "We're the same," he'd told Eric.

Could that be true?

Eric spotted David Hallenback walking ahead of him. Then in darted Cody, slapping David on the back, saying, "Hey, Hallen*back*!"

Very clever, that Cody.

Weasel.

Eric fell in step with Hallenback. "Don't let him get to you," he advised.

Hallenback shot Eric a look of amazement. He sped up, as if to shake Eric, but Eric kept pace. They were both headed to music class, on the far side of the building, so there was a long way to go. "I know how it feels," Eric confided. "You don't have to take it from those guys."

"Yeah, right," Hallenback mocked. "You know how it feels."

Eric looked at Hallenback out of the corner of his eye. He had a nervous, twitchy manner, always blinking, as if an anvil were about to drop out of the sky.

"You could talk to somebody," Eric said.

"Like that's going to help," Hallenback answered scornfully. "Listen, *friend*"—his voice was filled with sarcasm—"I'm no rat. I'm not crying to any teachers— and you're not, either."

"Hey, don't get so mad," Eric said. "I'm just trying to help."

Hallenback held up a fist in front of his chest, showing it to Eric. He extended his index finger, then his thumb. The sign was unmistakable. It was a gun. Hallenback pointed his finger at Eric, then lifted it to the ceiling, then twice pressed down his thumb. *Bangbang.* "I know how to defend myself," Hallenback said. "Don't worry about me, *friend*."

Eric tried (and failed) to concentrate on his homework during home base. For starters, there was a commotion in the back of the room, between Mary and some of the girls. It was some kind of disagreement. Mary stormed to Mr. Scofield's desk and demanded a pass to the library. Mr. Scofield refused. Mary protested, insisted it was important. Mr. Scofield held firm. Finally, after some hushed debate, he reluctantly made out a pass. "Thanks," Mary said, plucking the pass from his fingers.

"You're welcome, Mary. Good luck."

Something was definitely up.

Meanwhile, Eric had David Hallenback to worry about. The kid was starting to scare him. The whole "bang-bang" thing was just too weird. But what did it mean, really? David didn't make a threat. He didn't have a real weapon. It was just words, bluster from a boy who couldn't hurt a fly. Right? It's not like he threatened to hurt anybody.

The worst part of it, the guilty part, was Eric could totally see why some kids picked on Hallenback. The honest truth? There was something unlikable about that kid. Even though Eric tried to be decent to Hallenback, he kept pushing Eric away. Maybe that was for the best.

After stewing on this for a long while, Eric reached a decision. He pulled up a chair next to Hallenback. "Tell me one thing," Eric demanded, "and I won't bother you again. Why do you even *want* to be friends with Griffin and those guys?"

David stared levelly at Eric. "I *am* friends with them."

Eric was dismayed. "David, all they do is pick on you."

"Not always," he replied. "Griffin likes me."

Eric paused a beat, disbelieving his ears. "Griffin," Eric finally exclaimed in frustration, "is a bad guy!"

It startled Eric to hear himself say it out loud. Eric wasn't even sure he had thought it until the words sprang from his mouth. It was a gut feeling, rising up from deep down.

Griffin is a bad guy.

David Hallenback didn't answer. He went fish-eyed, shut his mouth, and nodded slightly—but not in agreement. The nod suggested something else, like David was making an internal decision, looking at Eric as if for the first time, and now thinking things through.

Eric had no idea what any of it meant.

20
[out]

ERIC SAT AT THE FAR END OF THE TABLE DURING LUNCH.
He had moved his seat away from Griffin after that
business with Hallenback in the playground. Eric
sensed that something was up. Not by how people
looked at him—no, that wasn't it—but by how they
didn't look at him. Griffin, Cody, all those guys. It
was as if Eric no longer existed. He was relieved when
the students were allowed to head outside for recess.

He felt worked up and edgy, his head a jangle of
different thoughts, all of them focused on Griffin

Connelly. So Eric drifted around the school yard, half looking for Mary.

She was alone, like him. "What's going on?" he asked.

Mary turned her head and stared. Eric followed her eyes and saw Chantel Williams standing with a couple of other girls. Chantel was crying, her body heaving, while the girls tried to console her.

"They got her, huh?"

"Didn't you see it?" Mary asked.

Eric had not.

"Alexis and the others posted a page on the Web. They sent e-mails out to a ton of people, linking to the page. It had all these horrible pictures of Chantel and it read, 'Ten reasons why Chantel Williams is a fat . . .'"

Mary didn't finish the sentence. She just swallowed in bewilderment, glancing around like someone who had lost her way.

"Does she know who did it?"

There was no reaction on Mary's face, just a flicker in her eyes. "The school knows. The resource officer, Mr. Goldsworthy, he knows."

Eric watched her closely. "You told?"

"I'm standing here alone, aren't I?" Mary said. There was a catch in her voice.

"You're not alone," Eric corrected her.

"Sorry, you know what I mean."

But Eric could see that Mary was right. Even though he stood beside her, inches away, she was isolated and alone. Mary wasn't "in" anymore. She had been pushed out.

Eric glanced across the school yard and saw a curious partnership. There was Griffin Connelly, walking along in close conversation with David Hallenback. They were set apart from everyone else, just two boys walking, hanging out. Griffin was nodding, listening. David seemed to be doing all the talking.

Strange.

Mary took a deep breath. "I'm going to talk to her."

"Chantel?"

Mary nodded. "I have to."

So once again Eric found himself at loose ends. More out of habit than anything else, he joined a loose cluster of the usual suspects: Drew P., Sinjay, Will, Hakeem, a few others. Inspired by Mary's stand against her friends, Eric abruptly asked, "Why do we let them get away with it?"

"What?"

"Bullies," Eric said. He was thinking about the presentation Mr. Floyd gave to the science class, of Chantel Williams and David Hallenback. "Why do we stand around and let it happen?"

They looked at Eric as if a yellow daffodil had sprouted from the top of his head.

"Dude, we're talking about the NFL," Drew P. said. "Hakeem says this is going to be the Jets' year."

Pat Daly laughed. "Hakeem *always* thinks it's going to be the Jets' year!"

"And this year I'm finally going to be right!" Hakeem bellowed, wagging a finger, flashing a toothy smile.

"I mean it," Eric persisted, refusing to be dragged off topic. "Like the other day with Griffin and David. Why didn't we do anything to stop it?"

The mood of the group changed, grew quiet and uncomfortable. A few sets of eyes looked away, perhaps searching for Cody and Griffin.

"What about it, Hakeem?"

The thick-bodied, dark-skinned boy stared at Eric. He smiled, lifted up his hands. "My parents tell me to stay out of it," he admitted. "I don't want any trouble."

"Hallenback is a loser," Drew P. interjected. "You know how annoying he is, Eric. That kid deserves a little roughing up now and then. It's like he asks for it."

"Please, sir, may I have another?" Marshall Jenkins joked in a whiny voice.

Most of the boys laughed, nodding in agreement.

Eric noticed that Pat Daly wasn't laughing.

"What about you, Pat?" Eric asked.

Pat swallowed, looked at the ground. "Even if, let's say, maybe you saw something that seemed a little harsh," he tentatively began. "What if you did say something? You'd get your butt kicked the next day."

"It's not worth it," another commented.

"Besides, who are you going to tell?" Marshall asked. "The principal? Mrs. Morris can't do anything."

"What about Officer Goldsworthy?" Eric wondered.

"No way I'd ever rat someone out," Sinjay stated. "Especially not to a rent-a-cop."

"Eric, listen to me, okay? You've got to lighten up,

dude," Drew P. advised. "Why make a big deal out of it? Okay, a few little things have happened. There's always going to be some guys who take a pounding. That's life. What do they call it in science? Natural selection," he pronounced.

Cody joined the group, stood close to Eric, practically breathing in his ear. Cody didn't say a word, but he listened hard, his body coiled, leaning in on the balls of his feet, like an unspoken threat.

Eric shook his head. "No, Droop. I don't think that's a fair—"

"Hey, guys! What are you talking about?" It was Griffin Connelly. His tone was cheerful, innocent. His eyes roved from one boy in the group to another, finally settling on Eric. "Huh, Eric?"

"Nothing, Griff," Eric murmured.

"All right, then," Griffin replied. He probed around the edges of his eye with a thumb, flicked away the offending dust particle. Everyone watched him, waiting uneasily. Griffin cupped his mouth with a hand and whispered to Eric, "Just be careful what you talk about," he warned. "It's hard to keep secrets around here."

Griffin winked at Eric. Then gave that big Hollywood smile, and swept the hair from his eyes.

The bell rang, the group began to disperse. Griffin tugged on Eric's shirt. "Hey, by the way, Eric, I listened to that CD of yours. I have to tell you, buddy, very weak. Those were some lame tunes. What is your father, a florist or something?"

Hearing it, a few boys laughed. Eric's face flushed.

"Oh no, I remember now," Griffin said, gleefully wagging a finger. "He's a freak."

For that moment, Eric's senses shut down. Instead of sight, the world went dark, like a curtain falling across his eyes. Instead of sound, he heard only the mad pounding of his heart, the soggy swoosh of blood running through his body.

Fists clenched, he wanted only to lash out, to hit something, to make it hurt.

"What are you going to do? Punch me?" Griffin taunted, grinning. "Don't you know that violence never gets you anywhere?"

Cody stepped in close.

Eric shook his head, the fury passed. They had attracted the attention of Mrs. Diaz and another noon aide. "You're not worth it," Eric declared.

Griffin, aware of his audience, held out open palms. "Dude, look at me. I'm just a guy who's standing here. You are the one who is all hot and bothered. The guy you really want to punch is your old man."

"*Bwawk-bwawk*, chicken," Sinjay clucked, still eager to see a fight.

"I'll be seeing you around, Eric," Griffin said. His smile was like a pure beam of distilled sunlight. His long lashes blinked, his cheeks pinkened. He wore a perfect mask of kindness and light.

21

[crossed]

DAVID WAS WAITING AT ERIC'S LOCKER WHEN THE FINAL bell rang. Hallenback seemed apprehensive. He bit his lip and looked from side to side, as if worried that someone might be watching. He was a boy who had grown used to being ambushed.

"What's up?" Eric asked.

"I've been thinking about what you said."

"Yeah."

"And I have to show you something," Hallenback said.

"Okay. Show me."

"I can't, not here," Hallenback answered. There was anxiety in his voice. He seemed fidgety, nervous. "I need to bring you there."

Eric frowned. He didn't have time for this. He had two dogs to walk when he got home, a mountain of math homework, plus an English paper to finish. "Can we make it fast?"

Hallenback chewed on his lip some more. He nodded sharply, not quite looking at Eric.

Eric sighed, dialed in his locker combination, grabbed his backpack, and they headed out the main door. Hallenback pointed toward the Final Rest Pet Cemetery. "In there," he said. "I don't want anybody else to see."

Eric started to complain. "This is dumb. Why do we have to . . . ?" But he stopped himself when he saw the expression on Hallenback's face. This was important to him. For the first time, battered and bullied David Hallenback was showing trust in somebody. Of all the people in Bellport Central Middle School, Hallenback reached out to Eric. Maybe that made sense, since Eric was still the new kid in town. Eric had tried to be nice to David lately. In some ways, he was just as much an outsider as David.

As they walked, Eric wondered what it could be that Hallenback wanted to show him. Something he found? A note? A photograph? Then the thought struck him— a weapon of some sort? A knife? A gun? Isn't that what happens when kids get picked on too much? Sometimes they can't take it anymore. And they break.

No, that wasn't it. Not Hallenback. But try as he might, Eric couldn't completely push the thought away. When it came down to it, Eric didn't know much about David Hallenback. Except that he was a perfect target, picked on every day, and angry most of the time.

They hopped a short fence and entered the grounds.

"Where are we going, exactly?"

"It's back here. You'll see."

Despite its proximity to the school, this was actually Eric's first time inside the cemetery grounds. It wasn't that creepy, the way a real cemetery—a *human* cemetery—could sometimes be. Eric couldn't get too worked up about a dead Siamese cat. Still, he marveled at the size of some of the headstones. There were a few that were really huge. Most of the gravestones were modest in height, about thigh-high, but they were thick and looked heavy. They were light brown or gray, with a few shiny black ones sprinkled in. Each had the pet's name engraved into it, complete with year of birth and death, and the last name of the owner.

Eric thought it was kind of comical. It was a cemetery, and that's serious stuff, but the names on the tombstones were, like, Sparky and Mugsy and Luther and Bubbles.

A few had pictures of the (dead, buried, rotting) pet, and there were even little statues of dogs and cats at some of the grave sites. Eric noticed fresh flowers at a couple of sites and that gave him a chill, the thought of some lady weeping at a grave site over poor old Mr. Chuckles, the world's perkiest Yorkshire terrier.

He thought of Mrs. Rosen, the lunch aide whose dog died over the summer. When she had talked to Griffin that day, she seemed really heartbroken over it. Maybe her dog was buried in here somewhere. What was its name? *Daisy.* He remembered something his father said, back a few years ago when Eric was lobbying hard for a pet. Eric's dad replied, "Dogs are built-in heartbreak. Ten good years, two bad years, some giant vet bills, then they die and break your heart. It's not worth it, believe me."

That was sooo his father. Mr. Half Empty.

"I wish I had a dog," Eric said.

Hallenback remained quiet, distant. He hadn't said a word since they'd entered the cemetery. Something on his mind, Eric surmised.

When they neared the far corner, Hallenback steered them to a low, granite tombstone. Several small American flags—the type that kids wave at Fourth of July parades—were planted in the ground at each side of the site. The tombstone read: CHECKERS, 1951–62, NIXON.

"Is this it? This is what you wanted to show me? Where President Nixon's dog is buried?"

Hallenback appeared distracted, not listening. He was looking off in the other direction. A group of five boys emerged from the far side of the cemetery.

Eric knew each one of them. They were led by Griffin, with Cody at his side. By the look on their faces, Eric could see they meant trouble.

Hallenback was going to get creamed.

"You'd better get out of here," he said to David. "Maybe I can talk to them."

But Hallenback snorted, a sound of disgust. He took a few steps closer to the approaching boys. "Hey, guys," he said.

"David," Eric warned. "Don't."

Hallenback lifted his head and stared at Eric. The look on his face was pure, unabashed disgust. "You stupid idiot. You think he's after me, don't you?"

It took a moment for it to register. Eric looked from Hallenback to Griffin, to Cody's hatchet face. A hollowed-out feeling entered Eric's chest, like a balloon expanding. An electric current tingled through his fingers, his legs felt leaden.

Oh, crap.

22
[boot]

CODY MOVED AGGRESSIVELY FORWARD. HE WAS ON EDGE, hyper, dangerous. He stood directly in front of Eric, too close for comfort. The others drifted nearer, forming a loose semicircle that faced Eric. Drew P. was there, with Will, and Sinjay, too. His so-called friends, here for the show.

Hallenback crossed an imaginary line and now aligned himself with Griffin, who greeted him with a subtle nod. Eric understood that something significant had happened. David Hallenback—of all people—had lured him off school grounds. It had been a trap. And it was here, Eric realized, where it was going to happen.

He looked at Hallenback. "Is this what you wanted to show me, David?"

"No, I've got something *I* want to show you!" Cody leaned in close. He put a hand on Eric's chest. "I heard what you said about me, Hayes." There was fury in his voice.

Eric didn't understand. "What I said . . . ?"

"What you called me." Cody tapped his knuckles on Eric's chest, not hard, but not soft, either.

Cody didn't want to say it out loud.

Not in front of everybody.

For the sliver of an instant, Eric wondered how Cody found out. He had said it out loud only once, and that was over a month ago, at the supermarket with Griffin.

Griffin. He was the one. Had to be. Griffin was the puppet master, pulling the strings without even lifting a finger. Griffin had arranged it all. Cody was just a tool, a weapon that Griffin used whenever he wanted.

Eric smirked. At that moment, he hated Cody's

face, hated his horse teeth, his ragged hair, everything about him. "What's the matter?" Eric said. "You don't want everyone to hear your new nickname?"

Eric paused, stared hard at Griffin, whispered it. "Weasel."

Cody's eyes blazed and he hit Eric on the side of his face with a ferocious right hook.

Eric staggered back, but did not fall. "I don't want to fight you, Cody," he said.

"I don't think you have a choice," Griffin noted from the sidelines.

Eric turned to walk away. Isn't that what you were supposed to do? The easy advice they give you. Just walk away.

When Cody reached for him, grabbed him hard, a switch went off in Eric's head. He turned and swung wildly. Cody ducked the blow and danced out of the way.

"Fight!" someone cried.

"Do it, do it!"

The others moved in closer, like sharks circling a swimmer. Blood was in the water.

Whoever taught Cody how to fight deserved a lot

of credit. Those karate classes really paid off. After a rapid flurry of punches, he grabbed Eric in a headlock and twisted, twisted, twisted until Eric was on his knees, fearing that his neck might snap.

He clawed at Cody's fingers, desperately trying to pry them apart. It was getting hard to breathe.

That's when punches rained down upon Eric's face. All left hands, hard and true.

At a certain point, it became a blur.

The whole fight—if you could call it that— probably lasted less than three minutes.

Eric was on the ground, gasping heavily on his hands and knees, spitting blood.

"Okay, Cody. You're done," Griffin said.

"Consider that a lesson," Cody said.

The others murmured, disturbed and excited. It was a chilling display of pure animal violence.

And it thrilled them.

Eric had only wanted it to end. And now he regretted, more than anything, his one punch that hadn't landed. If only he could have had the pleasure of cracking Cody in the face, just once, to feel his fist crunch against Cody's cheekbone.

Griffin bent over and plucked something from the ground. It was a little American flag from Checkers's grave.

Eric understood the gesture: Griffin needed his souvenir.

The party was over. But no one told David Hallenback.

Two feet stepped close to Eric's head. "You think you are so much better than me, don't you?" Hallenback spat. There was anger in his voice. So much pain bubbling up to the surface.

"I don't—" Eric gasped.

"Now you know what it's like!" Hallenback screamed. "Now you know!"

Hallenback had worn hiking boots that day, Eric noted, not the sneakers he usually wore. Special occasion, Eric guessed. And now Eric watched the boot lift, swing forward, and drive into his stomach.

Eric absorbed the blow, crumpled like a paper cup. He felt the cool earth on his face. It was nice, like a damp towel. Eric tasted grass, and dirt, and a warm trickle of blood from his lips.

Hallenback kicked a few more furious times. He

wasn't practiced at it, though, and the kicks were only glancing blows. Eric covered up, hands wrapped tightly around his head, body in a ball. He refused to cry out. No sobbing, no pleas for mercy. He took it in silence. But—*ungh*—that last kick knocked something out of him. His body grunted, heaved, constricted in pain.

"That's enough," Cody barked. "Leave him alone, Hallenback. He's down."

Eric heard them walk away. And a sound came up from his throat and passed through his lips. Laughter, except it hurt his ribs. Still, it *was* funny, though, when he thought about it.

David Hallenback had found a way to belong.

He was one of the gang.

All it took was kicking Eric's ass.

For a while—one minute, two minutes, five minutes—Eric just lay there, feeling oddly serene, wondering how badly he was hurt. He slowly stretched out his arms and legs. He ached all over. His neck was stiff. He felt his face. It seemed okay; only a little blood came off on his fingers.

Then he heard a bicycle pull up.

What now? Eric wondered.

"Are you okay?" Mary asked. She sounded frightened.

Eric half rolled to look up at her. Mary was standing with the sun behind her back, framing her head. Eric squinted; her face was in shadow, dizzying. "Oh, sure, I'm peachy," he said. Or maybe he just thought it.

"What?" Mary leaned down close, put a hand on Eric's shoulder, listened.

He shook his head. There really wasn't anything to say. It took too much effort anyway.

"I was hiding. I watched from the hill," she confessed. Her hands touched his face, wiped the hair from his eyes. "I waited for them to leave." She pulled at his arms and helped him sit. "It's not so bad. I've seen worse—but only in slasher movies."

Eric snickered at that.

And after a while, with her help, he stood.

"Let's get you home."

And somehow, together, that's what they did.

23
[unsent]

ERIC PLAYED A LOT OF GUITAR DURING THOSE DAYS. IT was the best thing for him, just losing himself in the instrument, slamming out fat chords, but mostly, not thinking.

He had written a letter to his father—the first one in a long, long time—and now it rested on the desk in his room.

Dear Dad,
     Hi, it's Eric.
     I guess you know all about us living on

Long Island. I like parts of it, and other parts are kind of weird. The ocean is cool. School is a little crazy.

It's hard being in a new place, you know? I had some friends but now I know they weren't my friends after all. So I'm kind of starting all over again at zero. Or one, maybe, but that's a long story. The truth is, I got beat up the other day. Don't worry. I'm okay. It wasn't so bad. I mean, sure, it totally sucked. So I spend a lot of time trying to forget all about it. Some days it works.

Is that how it is for you?

I'm sorry I didn't talk to you on the phone the other day. Don't be mad at me. Sometimes I just do things. It's hard to explain why.

I listen to your CDs a lot. I close my eyes and turn the music up loud. There's that song by Jimi Hendrix when the guitar goes whoosh from the left ear to the right ear and then back, like it's whipping through

my skull. Pretty cool. The other day I
thought of you and for a minute I couldn't
remember your face. It scared me. I have a
picture of you inside my desk drawer. I had
to go and look at it. It's from that time
when I beat you at putt-putt golf. I was so
happy that day. It was when we were on
vacation by the lake. Remember that? I do.

    I think I'm going to ask Mom for a frame
and hang that picture on my wall. I think
about you a lot. I still have that guitar you
gave me, but I mostly play the electric now.
I just learned how to play "Ziggy Stardust."
It's a cool song . . . Ziggy played guitar! You
are right about what you said. *Music helps.*

    Rudy is doing great. He's getting good at
sports. I never let him beat me, but
sometimes I let him come close. I might try
out for the school basketball team. I've been
practicing a lot, dribbling with both hands,
shooting jumpers from behind the line. I
really, really hope I make it.

Anyway, I don't know. I just wanted to say hi. And I'm sorry. I guess that's what we both do. We keep saying I'm sorry.

I miss you.

Love,
Eric

P.S. Did you know that President Nixon's dog is buried out here? How weird is that? He's the one that robbed the hotel, right? Or something like that!

It was a stupid letter, Eric decided upon rereading it, *and I never should have written it in felt marker.* Eric ripped it up and let the pieces flutter into the wastebasket, like snowflakes falling into a dark, deep well.

And so he picked up his guitar, plugged in the headphones, and started strumming.

24
[fallout]

MRS. HAYES'S INITIAL REACTION WAS SHOCK. AFTER ALL, her son had been beaten up in a pet cemetery. It was not the kind of news a mother hears every day. So she freaked.

Eric couldn't blame her. He did look like a mess. Before they reached Eric's house, Mary had helped him clean up in the bathroom at McDonald's. She went right in the men's room with him, just locked the door and went to work, dabbing and rinsing and making a fuss. Eric's face was bruised and swollen around the eyes and cheek. His lower lip was split. His body was sore, stiff, and bone tired. Nothing that two Advils every four hours, with a full weekend of rest, couldn't cure. His body would recover.

Mrs. Hayes asked a million questions, and when she didn't like the answers, she picked up the phone and started dialing. Eric, for his part, downplayed everything. At first he hoped to claim it was all a football injury, but after he looked at his face in the mirror, he knew the story wouldn't fly. So he spooned out a watered-down version of the truth—it wasn't that big of a deal, just a misunderstanding, and so on and so forth—but his mother took everything superseriously. She wanted names, she wanted facts. She was like one of those detectives on *Law and Order*. She even asked, "Checkers's grave site? Why is Nixon's dog buried in Bellport?"

Mrs. Hayes was not the type of person to let this kind of thing fade into the background, as Eric had hoped. She talked on the phone with school counselors, teachers, and the principal. She turned everything into a big deal. For Eric, that was the worst part of it. Being at the center of all that hand wringing. He just wanted it to go away. At the same time, a part of him was relieved. He was glad the school knew, that eyes had been opened, that this thing (supposedly) wouldn't happen again.

Eric managed to keep David Hallenback's name out of it. He had to tell about the other guys: Cody, Griffin, Drew, Will, and Sinjay. Maybe not telling the whole truth was a mistake. Maybe he should have said something about Hallenback. But some instinct told Eric to leave it alone. He wouldn't have said anything about Mary, either, except she insisted on waiting with Eric until his mother came home from work.

That was the first thing Eric said, after his mother exclaimed, "Eric, oh my God, what happened?"

He gestured feebly with his hand and said, "Mom, this is Mary O'Malley." It wasn't really a great time for introductions. But what are you going to do? It was not a perfect world, as Eric had resoundingly discovered.

"The dogs!" Eric suddenly remembered. He'd forgotten all about his dog-walking duties. Mary volunteered to do it. Eric wasn't sure.

"No," Mrs. Hayes cut in. "I'll take care of the dogs."

"Then I'll wait here with Eric," Mary said, and

there wasn't a trace of question in her voice. She wasn't asking permission.

"Fine," Mrs. Hayes relented. "I'll be back soon. There's some ice cream in the freezer."

Eric was sullen and embarrassed to be alone with Mary, and in such sorry shape. He was relieved when his mother returned and Mary left.

But she stopped by the next day. To drop off a video, she said. It was *The School of Rock*, starring Jack Black. Eric had seen the movie a few times already—"I pledge allegiance . . . to the band . . . of Mr. Schneebly . . ."— but it was the thought that counted, and to Eric it counted a lot. Seeing Mary was good, though, because now more than ever he felt cut off and alone.

Eric hated that first day back at school on Monday. Everyone knew about the fight. There were no secrets in seventh grade, plus his face looked like a bruised peach. He wanted to stay home an extra day, but his mother wouldn't allow it. She was all about "getting back on that horse" and blah, blah, blah. There was no arguing with her.

Walking the halls, sitting in classrooms—from the way kids looked at him, you'd think that his hair had turned into live snakes. He was, as Sophie Cerrone said in French class, *"Le* freak *du jour."*

She was kidding. Eric hoped.

Mr. Floyd, the counselor, summoned Eric to a meeting in his office. Eric was instructed to bring his lunch. The invitation came as a relief, since it allowed Eric to put off for another day the discomfiture of the cafeteria.

Mr. Floyd rose and greeted Eric when he entered the office. He inquired how Eric was feeling, gestured to a chair. All very gracious and smooth. Eric glanced around the room. In addition to the usual setup of a big desk and high-backed swivel chair, Mr. Floyd's office included a round conference table, "to facilitate meaningful dialogue," no doubt. It was here where Eric now sat. Nothing much happened at first. Mr. Floyd busied himself with a folder stuffed with a notepad and papers. So Eric tore into his sandwich. Ham and Swiss on rye, with just a whisper of mustard. Not bad.

There was a knock on the door behind Eric. Mr. Floyd looked up and said, "Thank you for joining us, Cody. Please take a seat."

Eric's heart sputtered. Cody looked glum and distrustful. He set down his lunch tray and took a seat at the table as far from Mr. Floyd and Eric as mathematically possible, so that the three participants now represented the points of a perfect triangle.

"I realize this must feel awkward for you," Mr. Floyd began, "but I felt it was important to bring you boys together to discuss what happened after school on Friday."

Mr. Floyd ran a hand over his goatee and pursed his lips. "I understand punches were thrown."

Cody and Eric exchanged wary glances. Neither said a word.

"Because it was off school grounds," Mr. Floyd continued, as he looked from boy to boy, "there isn't much I can do in terms of punishment. But I do want you to know that you are . . . on . . . my . . . radar." He looked directly at Cody. "Do you know what that means?"

"That you'll be watching us?"

"Exactly right," Mr. Floyd answered. "I want your agreement right now. This ends here."

He tapped his finger on the desk along with each word. "This—*tap*—ends—*tap*—here—*tap*. Do you understand?"

Cody glanced at Eric, nodded.

"Eric?" Mr. Floyd asked.

"It's not up to me," Eric said. "I didn't start it in the first place."

"You did so," Cody retorted. "I just finished it."

Eric looked away, muttering soundlessly.

"Is there something you want to say, Eric?" Mr. Floyd asked.

"Not really."

"I mean, this is your chance," Mr. Floyd urged. "I'm not asking you boys to kiss and make up"— Cody and Eric both instantly frowned and rolled their eyes—"but this is a chance to clear the air in a safe, private environment."

Cody looked like he might say something, as if he was forming the sentence in his head, but it was Eric who spoke first. "Look, I should have never said that about you. It's not how I want to . . . act. I'm not proud of it. Sorry."

Cody swallowed, reached for a glass of water. "I got so mad when I heard it," he confessed. "I've been trying to control my temper. You know that, Mr. Floyd. I'm sick of getting in trouble. But the guys kept after me. They kept getting in my face, saying, 'Are you going to let him get away with it?' "

"The guys?" Mr. Floyd interjected. "Meaning, Griffin Connelly?"

Cody instantly realized his mistake. "Griffin didn't *do* anything," Cody corrected himself. "It was all on me. I threw the punches."

Eric raised a finger. "And I caught them."

It was funny. Everyone chuckled, even Mr. Floyd.

"Did Griffin encourage you to fight?" the counselor asked Cody.

Cody looked across the table at Eric, then back to Mr. Floyd. His face was a blank stare. "Nobody can make me do something I don't want to do," he said.

"Yes, I understand, Cody, but—"

Eric interrupted the counselor. "We're okay, Mr. Floyd. If Cody says this is over, then it's over. We both made mistakes." He reached out a hand, and Cody took it.

"Truce," they said.

"Listen to me, Cody," Mr. Floyd said. "I'll be speaking with your parents. I'm going to let them know what we've talked about. And I promise you, I'll be talking to Mr. Connelly, too. This kind of behavior is unacceptable. We won't tolerate it in this school. There will be consequences."

When the boys left the office, they headed to their lockers. Fifth period was almost over. When Cody stopped at a water fountain, Eric paused there, too.

"He used you, you know that, don't you?"

Cody looked up, eyes searching. "What happened between you and me, that was a fair fight. It was between us, and us only. I fight my own battles."

"Good," Eric replied. "Or in my case, not so good."

Cody grinned. "Yeah. And, um, listen. It was wrong what Hallenback did out there. He's a jerk. I didn't see him go after you until—"

"I'll be all right," Eric interrupted. "I can handle David Hallenback. He's not my main problem."

Cody stood motionless, then nodded slowly. "I hear what you are saying. . . ."

The bell rang and the hallway flooded with students. Cody and Eric went their separate ways. Both, somehow, felt a little better about things.

25
[misfits]

ON TUESDAY, ERIC GOT HIS FIRST VIEW OF DAVID HALLEN-
back in the lunchroom—sitting in Eric's old seat. It
was almost funny, except it seemed kind of pathetic.
Eric was reminded of that old expression: "Be careful
what you wish for, it might come true." Hallenback
had gotten what he wanted, a seat with the "in" crowd.
But just a passing glance told Eric that for David, nothing would change. In fact, it would probably get
worse. He didn't fit in over there. And it would never
last.

Still, despite recent events, Eric liked some of the guys at that table. They could be okay, if only they'd let themselves. Pat and Hakeem were really nice, and they hadn't been in the cemetery that day. Neither was Marshall. Drew, Will, and Sinjay were there, but Eric saw them as sailboats on the ocean. They just went whichever way the wind blew. They went to see a fight—because it was exciting, because it was something to do, because Griffin said it was going to be cool.

Eric saw Cody watching him from across the room. Cody sat in his usual place, across from Griff, who had his back to Eric. Something seemed different. Eric couldn't put his finger on it. Maybe it was just his imagination. Cody was sitting there, but it looked like his mind was somewhere else.

"Want company? Or is this your own private Idaho?" Mary asked.

Eric's arm swept across the empty table. "Sit anywhere you like."

"Thanks," Mary said, plopping down across from him. She unzipped a banana and broke off half in her hand.

"Why aren't you sitting at your regular table?"

"I'm not wanted," Mary answered. She chomped on the banana. "That's okay, I don't want them, either."

"This is over that thing with Chantel?"

Mary nodded. "I'm now considered a traitor."

"I guess it's just us, then," Eric said.

"You and me, brother," Mary said, tapping her chest twice and flashing a peace sign. "It's like the Island of Misfit Toys over here. We could start a new country. I'll let you be in charge of Homeland Security."

Eric felt the bruise on his cheek. "You might want to rethink that."

"On second thought, I guess you're right. Are you going to eat that?" Mary reached for half of Eric's sandwich and bit into it.

"Help yourself," Eric said.

"Just did, and it was delicious."

"Hey, did I tell you? My mom finally caved. She bought me a cell phone."

"Get out!"

"For real. It was one of the unexpected perks of getting beaten up. She thinks I'll be safer with a phone."

"Sure, if you hit 'em over the head with it."

Eric noticed a few people glancing over at them, heads turning, tongues wagging. "People are going to talk, you and me sitting together."

"Let 'em," Mary scoffed. "I'm so tired of what other people think."

"Yeah?"

"Yeah, I'm serious. I'm done worrying about what people like Alexis Brown think of me."

"When did you get so smart?"

Mary shrugged. "I had to do a lot of dumb things first. After a while, I decided to try a different approach."

"How's it working out for you so far?" Eric asked.

"The food's better," Mary said, twisting open one of Eric's Oreos. She turned serious. "Do you know what Mr. Scofield told me? He said not to listen when people say bad things about me. He said, 'You know, Miss O'Malley, it says more about who they are than it does about you.'"

"Not bad," Eric said.

"I thought so," Mary agreed.

Mrs. Rosen, the lunch aide, stopped by the table.

"We're starting a new country," Mary informed her. "Would you like to apply for asylum?"

"Actually, Eric," Mrs. Rosen said, "I was wondering if you are still in the dog-walking business."

Eric said that he was. At which point Mrs. Rosen went into great, gushing detail over her new puppy, little Annie, a King Charles spaniel. "Oh, she's just the cutest thing you've ever seen!" Mrs. Rosen exclaimed. "She's still a puppy. But full-grown, Annie will only weigh about fifteen pounds."

Mrs. Rosen told Eric that she had to fly to Florida for a few days to visit a sick relative. "I need someone who I can really depend on," Mrs. Rosen said. "I just can't bear putting Annie in one of those kennels."

"I'd love to do it," Eric said. "But I thought you usually hired Griffin for those jobs."

Mrs. Rosen shook her head no. "I may be getting old, but I'm not blind yet. Let's leave it at that."

Eric arranged to stop by her house before the weekend to pick up a spare set of keys.

When she left, Eric looked across the room to see Griffin Connelly turned all the way around in his chair, scowling at him. Once they got outside, Eric found out why.

"What was that all about with Rosen?" Griffin asked Eric, who was shooting baskets.

"Why do you care?"

"You owe me," Griffin said. "I almost got into big trouble because of you."

"What?"

"You and your mommy ratted me out. I had to do some fast talking."

Eric grabbed a loose basketball and tried hard to ignore Griffin.

Griffin blew the hair out of his eyes. "What did you tell them?"

"The truth," Eric replied. "I said you never touched me."

"Still, my PINS officer is going to have a cow."

"Your . . . what?"

"PINS officer," Griffin repeated. "Don't you know anything? PINS! 'Person in need of supervision.'"

"You got in trouble before, huh?"

Griffin dismissed the question with a wave. He

raked the hair from his face. "Rosen hired you, didn't she?"

Eric drained a long jumper. One of the guys, Pat, rebounded the ball and snapped a pass back to him. Courtesy shot. Eric put up another. *Swish*. Eric loved the sound of a ball shivering through a chain net. "Don't get too close," he chided Griffin, "or you'll get burned. I'm on fire."

"I'll find out one way or the other," Griffin said, still harping on Rosen. "I already have a pretty good idea. She just got a new designer dog. Is she going on vacation? You might as well tell me. It'll save time."

Mary turned up, taking a place at Eric's side. "Come on, Eric. Let's go. It smells around here."

"What is he, your new boyfriend?" Griffin snapped.

Mary made a face. "You're an idiot, Griff. You know that?"

"Shut it," Griffin answered.

"That's genius, Griff. You lay awake all night writing this stuff?"

Suddenly invisible, Eric watched the two glare at each other. There was definitely some history between them, bad blood. Eric spoke up. "Yeah, you got it right,

Griff. I'm taking care of Mrs. Rosen's dog. I guess she doesn't trust you anymore." He paused. "Go figure."

Griffin's face hardened. "I'll get you back."

"You don't scare me," Eric lied.

Griffin smiled wide, folded his hands together, and said in a soft voice, "We'll see about that."

He turned and walked away.

Neither Mary, nor Eric, followed.

But they watched him go. Both wondering what he'd do next.

26
[bike]

ERIC STARED AT THE RACK WHERE HE HAD PARKED HIS BI-cycle. His chain was still there, but it had been cut in half. His bike was gone. *Jesus H. Christ.* It was one of his father's expressions, and it entered Eric's mind of its own volition, like a seed that had been planted long ago and now suddenly sprang to flower. The father in his mind, he was always there, even when he lived one thousand miles away. Eric looked around, hoping against hope that it was only a prank. That he'd find his bike thrown under a bush or something.

No such luck.

"Is there a problem?"

Eric turned to Officer Goldsworthy, the resource officer, though all the kids referred to him as "the school cop." He wore a shirt and tie, not a police uniform; technically, he was a police officer who sometimes worked at the school. It was kind of confusing.

"Well, yeah, actually, there is," Eric admitted. He showed Officer Goldsworthy the cut chain.

"Do you have any idea who might have done this?"

"Yeah, I have a pretty good idea," Eric replied.

The man watched Eric and waited. His silence came as an unspoken question: *Who?*

"Griffin Connelly, most likely," Eric stated.

"Did anyone see him do it?"

Eric shook his head, defeated. "I don't think so."

"I've seen you two together. He's your friend, isn't he?"

Eric looked at Officer Goldsworthy. He was an imposing figure, solidly built. Eric could imagine him on a football field, terrorizing quarterbacks. Eric answered, "Used to be, maybe."

"I guess he had you fooled."

"I guess," Eric echoed.

"Guys like that, they can fool people. Sooner or later, though, folks tend to catch on," Officer Goldsworthy mused.

The officer put out his hand. "I don't think we've met. You're Eric Hayes, aren't you? I'm Bill Goldsworthy."

"How do you know me?" Eric asked.

"I try to know everybody around here," the man answered. "It's my job."

"I've heard about you," Eric admitted. "I'm friends with Mary O'Malley."

The cop nodded, tight-lipped. "I've gotten to know Mary pretty well this year. She's a good girl. I think she's really trying to turn things around."

The conversation returned to the missing bicycle. Eric needed to file a report. "I'll be stuck in juvenile court all morning. Stop by my office anytime after twelve tomorrow," the officer said. "I can help you with the forms. In the meantime, I'll put a call in to the precinct, see if anything's turned up."

"You think there's a chance?"

He shrugged. "It happens. But honestly? Not too often. Guys who take bikes usually strip them down, file off the serial numbers, repaint them, sell them. It's tough. But," he added, "this might not be that kind of theft."

"What do you mean?"

"This isn't how organized thieves—the kind who run bike rings—usually operate," Officer Goldsworthy said. "As far as I know, only one bike is missing. You told me that yours is a couple of years old, nothing special. And you already seem to have an idea who took it."

Eric noticed a group of kids filter out of the main doors. They had probably stayed late for yearbook committee or some other activity designed to look good on their transcripts. Mostly girls, they sprawled on the main steps, nearly all of them on cell phones, waiting for their parents to pick them up. Eric knew they saw him, too, talking with the school cop.

Eric decided to get out of there.

"Well, I've got to get going."

"Do you need a lift?"

"Nah, it's not that far. I can hoof it," Eric answered. "But thanks."

Officer Goldsworthy nodded, folding his arms

across a broad expanse of chest. "Listen, Eric," he began. "A word to the wise. There's been some burglaries in the community. Nothing too big, minor break-ins, things taken from parked cars. Small stuff." He paused. "You don't happen to know anything about that, do you?"

"Why would I know?" Eric replied. "I'm the guy who just got his bicycle stolen."

"Take it easy," the officer said. "I'm just saying that we're going to catch whoever is doing this. We always do. Keep your eyes open, okay? Let me know if you hear anything."

The two looked at each other, across a great silence. Eric thinking about Griffin Connelly, Officer Goldsworthy watching him think.

Eric pondered over Rudy's twenty-seven dollars, his father's CD, and that dark, wooden box of odd treasures up in Griffin's room. What did he say they were again? *His souvenirs.*

The faint stirrings of an idea swirled in Eric's mind. A plan.

27
[locker]

AFTER THINKING IT OVER ALL NIGHT, LYING IN BED STAR-
ing at the ceiling, Eric awoke on Thursday morning
with a clear decision in his mind. No way. It was too
risky. He couldn't do it.

But something happened at school to change his
mind.

The problem of Griffin Connelly wasn't going to
disappear on its own. Not unless Eric did something
about it. The stolen bicycle made that clear. In school,
Eric felt as if he had a target painted on his back. He
could tell from the way kids treated him, the watchful

distance they kept. A pressure was building, like air in an overinflated tire. Eric couldn't sit back and take it anymore. He had to act.

During social studies, Eric's second-to-last period of the day, Principal Morris came to the door. She asked for Eric to step into the hallway. Ominously, she told him to bring his books. Everyone turned to watch Eric leave. He was bewildered at first, but then he thought, *This must be about my bike.*

It wasn't. In the hallway, Mrs. Morris and Mrs. Ryan, the house leader, stood stone-faced. "Eric," Mrs. Morris said, "I'm afraid we received some information today that we are required to follow up on. We need to take a look inside your locker."

"My locker? I don't—"

"As you know, lockers are considered school property. We'd like you to come with us now."

"Yeah, sure."

No one spoke as they walked down the hall and down the stairs, echoing with the *click-tap* of Mrs. Ryan's shoes. Eric finally mustered the courage to ask, "What do you think I have in there?"

"A student came forward and reported that you had a knife," Mrs. Morris said. "We take those claims very seriously."

Eric was shocked. "A knife? I'd never bring—" He stopped walking. "Who said this about me?"

"Please," the principal said, gesturing with her arm. "Let's just get through this."

The hallway was deserted. Mrs. Ryan carefully searched his locker. She found an unholy mess, but no weapon. She pulled out Eric's backpack, handed it to Principal Morris, who zipped and unzipped every compartment.

Just then, Mary appeared from around the corner. "Eric? What's going on?"

"This is a private matter, Mary," Mrs. Ryan said. Her voice was firm. "Please return to your classroom."

Mary locked worried eyes with Eric. "But—"

"I'm okay," Eric said. "It's a mistake."

Mary nodded, still unsure. She turned and left.

Officer Goldsworthy met them outside the boys' locker room. Eric was relieved that Mrs. Ryan and Mrs. Morris didn't intend to go inside. The officer nodded a greeting, said softly, "Eric." He was in uniform today, probably because he was called over from the precinct.

By now, Eric felt more relaxed. "My locker is kind of gross," he half apologized.

If Officer Goldsworthy had a sense of humor, it was not currently on display. "Open it up, please."

The only possible weapon found inside Eric's gym locker was an old pair of white socks. Eric could have killed someone by holding the socks under their nose. Death by foot sweat.

For the final insult, Eric had to empty his pockets.

When they emerged in the hallway, Officer Goldsworthy nodded at Principal Morris. "False alarm," he said.

She nodded, smiled briefly at Eric. "I'm sorry we had to put you through this," she apologized. "But I hope you understand that a weapons report is serious business."

Eric understood, but he refused to acknowledge it. Instead, he stood expressionless, his teeth clenched together. "You aren't going to tell me who said it, are you?"

The adults exchanged glances. "No," Principal Morris answered, "it's confidential. Otherwise, students might be reluctant to make a report."

"So will anything happen to him? I had to go through all this, be treated like a criminal, just because somebody lied. It's not right." Eric worked to control his voice, but there was anger in it.

A few students began trickling into the halls. Mrs. Ryan checked her watch. "Seventh period should be out in a minute."

"Okay, Eric, you're free to go," Mrs. Morris said. "Please understand. This isn't a part of the job that I enjoy."

"Yeah, me, neither," Eric grumbled, heading off down the hall. He still had English with Mr. Scofield. Then finally he could go home.

A few kids from social studies—Pat Daly, in particular—were eager to ask about what had happened. Eric wasn't in the mood, so he lied, made up something about a sick relative and kept it short. He barely listened during English. *Who was behind it?* he wondered. Griffin Connelly was the easy answer. But the report might not have come from him. That wasn't

Griffin's style. He'd goad someone else into doing it. Eric thought of the Dare game, and of David Hallenback, and Cody, and his stolen bicycle. His body vibrated with anger, knees pumping, feet tapping. Why would Griffin, if it *was* Griffin, put Eric through that? Just to embarrass him?

"Eric?" a voice spoke. Then louder: "Mr. Hayes?"

"Wha—?"

"Would you mind returning to this planet?" Mr. Scofield admonished. "Take out your book. Page one hundred and sixteen, please."

Eric glanced around the room. Everyone had their novels out. "Oh, sorry," Eric mumbled. But even with the book opened to the right page, his thoughts journeyed elsewhere.

28
[confession]

MARY CAUGHT UP WITH ERIC AS HE LEAPED DOWN THE FI-
nal four steps. A long row of yellow school buses, like
a line of enormous Twinkies, idled along the right side
of the parking lot.

"You're taking the bus today?" Mary asked.

"No bike. Too young to drive a car. You got any
better ideas?"

"We could walk," Mary suggested. "I want to talk
to you about something."

"All right," Eric answered, quietly pleased with the
new arrangement.

They walked a few blocks in the midst of assorted clumps of students, until the throng eventually thinned to nothing, leaving the street empty for Eric and Mary. "This way," Mary said, steering Eric to a little pocket park. It was only a small patch of grass and three stone benches, obscured by a row of tall bushes. But the place had a closed-in feeling, a little reprieve from the endless rows of tidy, aluminum-sided houses.

"Cool, I never realized this was here."

"It's where Griffin used to come to smoke cigarettes," Mary admitted, making a face to show how totally gross she thought that was. "It was during his Marlboro Man phase."

Griffin, Eric thought. The name that would not go away. He hated to hear it associated with Mary. He knew they had been friends, once. Maybe even better than that. After all, that's when he first saw Mary, that hot summer day on the basketball court. It was autumn now, the leaves had changed, and the nights were colder. Still, Eric refused to wear anything warmer than a long-sleeved shirt. *Mary and Griffin.* It made Eric think about things he preferred to ignore.

Mary turned to him on the bench, her hands fidgeting on her lap. "Eric, I have to tell you something."

She seemed upset, intense. "What? Just say it, Mary."

"I knew about Cody."

"I don't understand."

Mary pressed on. "I knew what they were planning to do to you that day at the cemetery. *I knew it.* And I didn't say anything." The words flew out of her mouth in a fluttering rush, like doves escaping a coop, a feathery *whoosh* climbing to the sky.

"I don't—" Eric looked down, lifted his gaze back to Mary. There were real tears in her eyes. One fell down her cheek. He reached a hand toward her face.

"Don't," she said. "Just listen, all right?"

Eric nodded.

"I was afraid and I . . . and I'm just . . . really, really sorry."

Eric didn't know what to say. He felt betrayed, like he'd been punched in the stomach.

"I knew it was wrong," she said, sniffling. "I'd heard those guys talking. But I was too much of a . . .

coward . . . to stand up to them. I could have warned you."

Eric leaned closer. "It's okay, Mary," he whispered.

She sighed deeply, cleared her throat, shook the cobwebs out of her head. Mary smiled, shyly, at Eric. A different smile than he'd seen from her before. He felt it in his fingertips. "When I saw you on the ground, and that idiot, Hallenback, kicking you . . ." Her voice trailed off. "I made a promise to myself that I'd never, ever do anything like that again."

"You didn't *do* anything. You didn't punch me, you didn't kick me. Those guys did it. Not you, Mary."

"No," Mary shook her head. "You're wrong, Eric. And that's why I had to tell you. I'm sick of everything. I don't want to be like them."

They sat together for a while longer, until it was time to go. Outside Mary's house, when it was time to say good-bye, Eric reached out for her hand, just held it because he didn't want to let go. She finally pulled away, said, "I'll see ya, thanks."

He watched her walk across the lawn to her front door. Mary stopped, hands deep in her pockets, and called back to him, "You're really sweet, you know that."

And she went into the house.

Eric stood and watched the red door close between them. A gust of wind swept leaves across the lawn.

Then: *Oh my God,* he remembered, *Mrs. Rosen! I was supposed to pick up her keys!* He set off down the street, running, his feet barely touching the pavement.

29
[threat]

ERIC HAD NEVER CONSIDERED HIMSELF A SMALL-DOG person. He preferred dogs that went *ruff-ruff*, not *yip-yip*. Eric liked dogs that he could wrestle—not trip over. But he had to admit: Little Annie, the purebred, brown-and-white King James spaniel, was pretty darn cute.

Mrs. Rosen hovered around the dog like a worried helicopter, fretting and fussing. She showed Eric a two-page list of typed instructions, complete with emergency phone numbers. Eric promised that he'd do a good job, stuffed the spare keys in his pocket, and left.

He didn't get far before a familiar voice called after him. "Errr-ic!"

It was Griffin Connelly, gliding toward him on a skateboard.

"Hey, *buddy*. I was wondering when you'd show."

"How'd you know I'd be here?"

"That would be giving away my secrets, wouldn't it?" Griffin answered evasively.

Eric resisted the urge, compelling as it was, to punch Griffin in the face. Partly because he knew it couldn't possibly end well, and there wouldn't be much pleasure in having his butt handed to him by Griffin Connelly. Perhaps he also heard the echo of Mr. Floyd's comments in the counselor's office that day. Violence wasn't the answer. Instead, Eric asked, "Did you steal my bike?"

"I don't know what you're talking about," Griffin answered. He looked Eric in the eye when he said it. Never batted an eyelash. If he was lying—and Eric felt certain that he was—then Griffin did it with untroubled ease. Deep down, Griffin didn't seem to care what Eric thought or felt. It was something he lacked, a hole in his core, some basic absence of human sympathy. Griffin didn't *feel* much of anything. He was cold and hard, a brick. It was the quality, Eric realized, that made Griffin so scary—far worse than being mean or angry. His heart was flawed, wounded in some horrible way.

"I had my locker searched today," Eric told him.

"Why are you looking at me like that?" Griffin taunted. "Is that your scary face, Eric? Am I supposed to get all nervous? You want to hit me, don't you? Go ahead, you can pretend I'm your dad. I'll give you one free shot."

"I don't hate my father," Eric said.

"Sure you don't," Griffin answered.

"I don't," Eric snapped. "And you're too stupid to understand."

Eric loosened his shoulders, unclenched his hands, tried to shake the tension out of his body. He started walking. In two blocks, he'd be home. "I don't want to talk to you."

"Oh, I think you're wrong about that, Eric."

Griffin glided across Eric's path. He stepped off, casually kicked the back end of the board, and up it popped into his hand. A cool trick. "So," Griffin said. "I want to make you an offer."

"Not interested," Eric said.

Griffin smirked, like a card player holding a full house. He absently massaged his chest with his right hand. "How'd that locker thing go, anyway? They find anything?"

Eric ignored him, kept walking.

"I didn't think so," Griffin continued, "or else you'd be way screwed. I hear you can get thrown out of school if they catch you with drugs or a weapon. It would be a real shame, Eric. I'd hate to lose you."

"What did you do?" Eric said. "Get David to make the report for you."

"Hallenback is a puppy," Griffin responded. "He'd jump off a bridge for me."

"He'll figure it out someday," Eric replied. "One of these days, you're not going to have any friends left."

Griffin snorted in a show of indifference. But Eric's words seemed to push him off balance. He responded by going on the attack. "You better be careful what you put into your locker, Eric. Next time, it could be a lot worse," Griffin said. "Do these numbers mean anything to you, good buddy? Thirty, twelve, twenty-six."

It was Eric's locker combination. A number that nobody but Eric was supposed to know. "How did you—?"

"I've got *friends,* unlike you," Griffin spat.

Eric thought of that day when Hallenback met him at his locker. How Eric was in a hurry. He carelessly opened and shut his locker with David at his side. Could Hallenback have gotten the combination that way? Then passed it along to Griffin?

"It would be easy for me to plant something in your locker. You know that, right?"

"What is . . . *wrong* . . . with you?" Eric asked, his voice rising in frustration. "Why can't you just leave people alone? Is your life so miserable that this is how you have to spend your time? You're a waste, you know that, a total waste."

Griffin grinned through the insults. "Oh, Eric. You are hurting my feelings. The deal is, I want you to do one thing for me. One little thing. And then I promise it will stop. I'll never bother you again."

Of course, Eric didn't believe him. But Griffin had piqued his interest. "What do you want?"

"A souvenir."

"What?"

"From Rosen's house," Griffin said. "I've been in there. Her husband has this big coin collection. They'll never miss it if you take a couple of old silver dollars."

"What are you talking about?"

"You have the keys, it'll be easy," Griffin urged, selling it with a smile. "When you are in there, look around, and take something for me. Nothing wrong with that. Consider it a payment. What's wrong? You don't have the guts?"

"Are you out of your—there's no way I'm stealing for you!"

"That was the wrong answer, Eric. But then again, you've always disappointed me. Ever since that day on the basketball court. Remember that foul shot? Air ball. You choked. Your father doesn't want you—and who could blame him. You're just a loser." He stepped closer to Eric, skateboard in his hands. Griffin raised the board as if to club Eric with it . . . and Eric flinched, took a step back. Griffin laughed. "Dude, why so jumpy?"

It was as if Griffin were playing him like a yo-yo, up and down, back and forth. Eric was tired of the game. "Get away from me," he said, pushing Griffin aside.

"You're a smart guy, Eric," Griffin called after him. "Figure it out. That house is loaded with stuff. Rosen's got way more than she deserves. You'll be like Robin Hood, Eric. Stealing from the rich . . . giving to Griffin Connelly! You come through for me, I'll never hassle you again."

Eric picked up his pace. He wanted to clamp his hands over his ears and run. Just run away. But he couldn't give Griffin that satisfaction.

"You're a smart guy," Griffin repeated. "Thirty, twelve, twenty-six. Do you really want it to go down that way?"

Eric kept walking, trying hard not to listen. He could get a new locker tomorrow. Yet Eric knew that Griffin would always be able to find a way to open it.

Even after Eric shut the front door, Griffin's laughter still echoed in his ears.

It had to stop.

Eric was a smart guy. Griffin said so himself. One way or the other, he'd figure it out.

30
[repairs]

ON SATURDAY, MRS. HAYES SHOOK ERIC AWAKE. "TEN o'clock," she clucked. "You can't sleep the day away."

She served French toast for breakfast, made with challah bread, Eric's favorite. He accepted it with a bleary-eyed grunt. He didn't feel like talking; instead, his dark thoughts dwelled on Griffin Connelly.

Mrs. Hayes sat down at the family computer. Eric watched her unhappily. "Why can't I use instant message?" he complained.

"Eric, we've been through this."

"Don't you trust me?"

"I trust *you*," his mother replied. "It's the Internet I don't trust. Turn sixteen and we'll talk about it."

She was right about one thing: They had been through this before. So Eric sat, stewing in silence. Which reminded him: "Where's Rudy?"

"He got invited to the Guillens'. It's the twins' birthday. They're driving out to the Hayden Planetarium, then going out for pizza afterward. He'll be gone most of the day."

Eric shoveled more French toast into his mouth.

"I was thinking we could go to the beach," Mrs. Hayes announced, rising to pour herself another cup of coffee. "Just you and me. We never get to spend time together anymore."

Eric glanced out the window. The day was overcast, windy, probably no warmer than fifty-five degrees. The thought of spending a day at the beach with his mother left Eric unenthused. "It doesn't look like beach weather to me."

"Oh, these are my favorite type of beach days," she said. "It's empty and peaceful. We'll have the place to ourselves. Come on, snap to it! Finish those strawberries, get dressed, and let's get a move on."

"Mom."

"Please, Eric," she said. "Enough with the grunts and brooding silences. Come on, let's go. Liven up! It'll be fun."

She was bound and determined to enjoy some "quality time" with her eldest son; Eric had no choice but to go along for the ride.

"Should we take our bikes?" she wondered.

The bike. Eric hadn't found the right time to tell her yet. "I have a flat tire," he said, making his best effort to appear downtrodden.

His mother snapped up the car keys. "That's fine— we'll get our exercise on the boardwalk."

They cruised along Wantagh Highway to Jones Beach, a long strip of gray-white sand beach that was divided into different "fields." Eric's mother parked at Field Four in one of the biggest, emptiest parking lots Eric had ever seen. There were only about a hundred cars there, but the place looked otherwise deserted. Eric glanced skyward; dark cumulus clouds loomed overhead, laden with rain. His mother led the way, a definite bounce in her step. "Growing up, this is where I often came to get away from everything," she confided to Eric. At their first glimpse of the ocean, she stopped and inhaled the salt air.

They stopped at a concession stand, Eric grabbing a Coke, his mother some fries. "Boy, this brings back memories," she gushed. "In high school, I worked all around here during the summers, mostly at West End Two and Field Six. You could get a job here in a couple of years, Eric. They are always looking to hire kids in the summer."

"Does it pay well?"

"Horrible! But it's so much fun. Those were great times."

They returned to the boardwalk, turned right, and headed west.

"Overcast and gloomy," his mother observed, sunshine in her voice. "It reminds me of Ireland. That's where your father and I honeymooned, you know. Dingle Bay. The Ring of Kerry. We even visited Yeats's grave in Sligo. I'd love to take you and Rudy there someday."

Eric wondered if she'd brought up the honeymoon on purpose. Now there it was, floating like a carnival balloon. The thought of his father. Eric asked her about it. What had happened, why his father never got better, why he didn't care anymore.

"Oh, he cares, Eric, don't ever stop believing that," she answered. "He loves you and Rudy very much."

"But why?" Eric asked, feeling it unnecessary to fill in the rest.

"When things got hard, he just wasn't equipped," she told her son. "He had difficulties—mental issues— that we kept under control with medication. But when he went off his meds . . ."

None of this was news to Eric. His mother had already told him everything, answered every question, countless times. Eric never understood why a sick person would stop taking medicine. It made no sense. But his mother said it was quite common, because most pills came with very unpleasant side effects. "I think your father started thinking he could handle it, you know, without the medicine. He kept hoping, you know. All he wanted was a normal life. So he stopped. I suspected, but he hid it from me. And after a while . . . he changed."

"I remember," Eric lamented.

"He did the best he could," his mother said. "He still does."

"Will he ever get better?"

Her lips tightened. She looked to the gray Atlantic. Seagulls wheeled near the surf, diving at the whitecaps. "I wish I could make it easier for you."

"But if he took his medicine—"

"It's not that simple," she replied. "The drugs dulled him. They controlled the bad parts. But they also carved away something from his spirit, the things that made him . . . *him*. You know?"

Eric didn't answer for a while. "I don't know if I'll ever understand."

"I know, honey," she said, and wrapped an arm around his shoulder. "But he's your father, Eric. You only get one in this life. All you can do is love him, even if it breaks your heart sometimes."

"I guess," he murmured.

She slipped off her shoes and stepped off the boardwalk onto the cool sand. "Come," she said.

"It's been a crap year," Eric confessed.

His mother held her hand flat above her eyes,

shielding them from the sun. "Are you gonna be all right?"

Eric nodded. "I think so, yeah."

She slipped her hand around his arm. "You are growing up, you know that?"

"Every day," Eric said.

"Just don't be in such a hurry. Hey, I've got an idea. See that building with the big glass windows? That's the Jones Beach restaurant. I haven't eaten there in years. Let's go eat some lobster. It'll be a treat. What do you say?"

"Lobster?" Eric repeated. "I'm always up for lobster."

LATER THAT AFTERNOON, WHEN THEY PULLED INTO THE driveway, Eric saw three boys knocking on the front door: Pat, Hakeem, and Cody. They had Eric's bicycle with them, lying on the front walkway. It was a crippled wreck, with bent forks and mangled tires.

His mother looked searchingly from the boys to the bicycle. "Eric?"

"I know these guys, Mom. It's okay. I got it."

His mother went inside, with just a sharp nod to the group. Eric stood eyeing the three boys.

"We were thinking, that is, me and Hakeem and Cody, that, um—" Pat floundered.

"We found out about what happened to your bike," Hakeem explained.

"It's not right," Cody stated, glancing down at Eric's feet. He looked up. "We told Griffin that he went too far."

"You did? How'd that go over?"

Hakeem smiled, tilted his chin to Cody.

"We kind of talked Griff into letting us take it back," Cody answered, rubbing the knuckles of his right hand. "It was their idea. I just came as backup."

"Did you have a fight?"

Cody shook his head. "No, no, we're still good. Griff and I have been friends for a long time. We just needed to air things out a little."

"Still," Eric said, "Griff must have been angry."

Hakeem glanced at Pat. "You know, in some ways, he didn't even seem surprised."

"We told him it wasn't funny anymore," Pat said.

"Wow, that's, like, really—thanks," a tongue-tied Eric replied. "I never expected this."

"We want to help you fix it," Pat piped up. "Do you have any tools in your garage? Otherwise, I've got some at my house. We could bring them back there."

"It's going to need a couple of new rims, probably new brake cables," Cody said, stepping toward the bicycle. "I think I can bend these forks back into shape, but it looks like the seat got slashed. I think I've got an extra one at my house. The derailer looks okay. . . ."

"Cody is an ace mechanic," Hakeem said. "He's going to build his own car someday."

Cody pulled a dirty bandanna from his back pocket to wipe the grease from his hands. "That's right. A Ford Mustang. You laugh now, but we'll see who's laughing when I'm—*eerrrrrrpp!*—chirping out, tires smoking, doing neutral drops in front of your house."

Hakeem and Pat laughed.

Cody looked at Eric, shrugged, palms up. "What can I say? I'm a motorhead. I've got three older brothers. We have a shed filled with old bicycles and spare parts. I think we can patch something together without too much trouble."

Eric listened to him with something close to amazement. When Cody talked about forks and brake cables and Ford Mustang carburetors, he was like a different person. A happier, more confident one.

Eric couldn't refrain from asking, "Why are you helping me?"

Cody took off his cap, scratched his head. "I like working on bikes," he said. "Besides, maybe after we get this piece of junk working again, you and me . . . we'll be even. Look, I don't know about you and Griffin, or you and Hallenback, or anything else like that. I'm not going there. I just want you and me to be square. Straight lines, you know. Leave the past in the past."

"Sounds good to me," Eric agreed.

Cody nodded, the business concluded. He said to Pat and Hakeem, "I'm going with Griff to see the car show tomorrow. My brother said he'd take us. You interested?"

The boys demurred, made excuses why not. Eric

sensed that it was Griffin's presence that put them off. Maybe that was just wishful thinking. Or maybe the tide was turning. Maybe things were going to change. The boys made arrangements to work on the bike sometime after school next week, Monday or Tuesday. It was up to Cody, really, since he was the one, as he said, "with the skills and the drills."

After they left, a semidazed Eric wandered around to the back of his house. A soft, cleansing rain began to fall. He hit speed dial on his cell phone.

"Hey!" Mary sounded happy to hear from him.

"You wouldn't believe who I was just hanging out with," Eric opened. Then he said, "Listen, are you going to be around tomorrow? I need your help with something. . . ."

Mary was dead set against it. But Eric was insistent. He was like his mother that way; his mind was made up.

Then the clouds broke, and buckets of rain poured from the sky.

31
[even]

ERIC FOUND THE NUMBER IN THE PHONE BOOK AND dialed.

"Yeah?"

"Um, hi, this is Eric. Is—"

"Griff! Phone!"

It was a male voice, the father.

"What?" It was Griffin now, but with the same unfriendly tone as his father.

"It's Eric."

There was a pause on the other end, a moment of silent appraisal. "So?"

"I need to talk to you. Can I come by tomorrow afternoon?"

"Unh-unh, mañana doesn't work," Griffin answered. "I'll be out most of the day."

It was the confirmation Eric needed.

"After dinner, maybe," Griffin suggested.

"Nah, never mind. It can wait."

"Oh no, you can't do that," Griff protested. "You called me, remember? Now you've got to say what it's about."

So Eric flat out let the words fly: "I'm not going to steal for you. It's a stupid idea."

"If that's the way you want it," Griffin said. "It's your life."

"I know about the break-ins," Eric said. He was bluffing now, playing a hunch. He didn't *know* anything, but he wanted to hear Griffin's response.

"What are you talking about?"

"You have to stop, Griffin," Eric warned him. "You'll get caught."

"Nope, I don't think so."

So there it was. Just as Eric suspected. Griffin

Connelly had graduated from stealing birthday money to petty burglary. It was more sad than surprising.

"Why do you care, anyway?" Griffin asked.

It was a fair question.

"Because I do," Eric answered.

"Sure, like I believe that."

Eric sighed. He suddenly felt tired, so tired. The seconds yawned past.

"Well," Griffin asked, "is that all you wanted to say to me?"

"That's pretty much it."

Griffin snorted. "And that's just lame, if you ask me."

"I guess I'm lame, then," Eric said with a shrug in his voice. "See you around, Griff."

Click.

ERIC MET MARY AT ONE O'CLOCK THE NEXT AFTERNOON, down the block from the Connellys'. They slowly walked past the house. "Driveway is empty," Eric noted. "I don't see any lights on. Nobody's home."

"Eric," Mary said. "This is such a bad idea. I mean, in the history of bad ideas, this is right up near the top, next to, like, I don't know, veggieburgers and spandex unitards."

Eric smiled, not dissuaded. "I have to do this. He stole something from my brother, and something from me. I want it back."

"It's just money, Eric. And a stupid CD—you can burn another one."

"It's more than that, Mary," Eric answered. "I *need* to do this."

"And if you get caught?"

"I won't," Eric promised. "Griffin will be gone all day. I called the house five minutes ago. No one's home. I'll be in and out. Besides, I've got you on lookout."

"I'm going to ring the bell, just to be sure," Mary said. And she did, marched right up there, and rang more than once. No one answered. Mary seemed disappointed.

"Griff once told me they always leave the back door open," Eric said.

Mary nodded in agreement. She knew the same

thing. "Before you go in, check the garage. Make sure the car isn't parked in there."

The house had a detatched garage behind the house, at the end of the driveway. Eric glanced toward it, distracted, and nodded.

"Wait! Give me your cell phone," Mary said.

"Why?"

"Just do it," Mary demanded, holding out her hand. She punched her phone number into Eric's cell, answered her phone, then hit the mute button. "Here." She handed his cell back to him. "Now we're connected. It's a one-way intercom. If you have any problems in there, just give a shout. I'll hear you."

"Okay, cool."

"I saw it in a movie once," Mary explained. "But everybody in it died anyway."

"Nice," Eric murmured. He jerked his head down the road. "And what about—"

"If anybody shows up, I'll be doing push-ups on the doorbell," she promised.

Eric turned to leave.

"Eric, please. This doesn't prove anything," Mary pleaded.

"Sorry."

The back door opened soundlessly. Eric stepped into the house and waited, every muscle taut, like he was five years old again and caught in a game of Freeze Tag. The door had opened into the kitchen. Dishes were piled in the sink, the morning paper was on the table, open to the funny pages.

The coast was clear. Eric silently made it to the main hallway, then up the stairs. His body quivered, fingers trembled. He wanted this to be over as quickly as possible.

When he reached the top step, Eric heard it: one loud, thunderous snore. Then silence.

Eric pinned himself to the wall, like an exotic bug with a needle stuck through it. He didn't move, he didn't breathe. The snore came from a bedroom down the hallway. Eric peeked around the corner; the door was ajar. It must have been the master bedroom. Mr. Connelly was in there, sleeping off a night shift.

Another great, gasping snore shook Eric's insides. His stomach did cartwheels. *Idiot,* he cursed himself. In his haste, Eric had neglected to check the garage and now he was paying the price. But instead of leav-

ing immediately, just easing down the stairs and slipping out the front door, Eric waited, paralyzed.

The snoring was unvarying, on and off in regular intervals.

Eric hesitated at the top of the stairs, trying to make a decision. Directly opposite him, there was a bathroom. The snoring came from a room to the left. The other door was probably a linen closet, Eric figured. Griffin's door was five feet to Eric's right. *Screw it,* Eric decided, mustering his courage. This would only take a minute.

Once he stepped inside Griffin's room, Eric untied his sneakers and set them down on a dresser. He moved purposefully to the wooden box that Griffin had shown him on Eric's first visit to the house. "My souvenirs," Griffin had called them. Eric realized what they were, little keepsakes, mementos of past triumphs. A pin lifted from the jacket of another student, a tooth knocked out in a fight, a small American flag taken from a dog's grave, various hood ornaments snapped off cars, small items from the cars he burglarized, a bunch of old coins, and more.

The guy was as sentimental as a punch in the face.

There was a fat wad of cash, rolled up in a rubber band. Eric unrolled the money, counted out twenty-seven dollars, replaced the wad—now a touch lighter—and returned the box to its exact spot on the shelf.

He glanced around the room. *Where's the CD?* Eric found a disordered stack by the bed stand, a random clutch of music. Eric wondered if they had all been stolen—a tough way to put together a good collection. He found the slim, homemade case to his father's CD. It was empty. Next to the iHome, there was a small CD player. Eric stealthily moved to it, pressed the open button. And there it was, the CD his father had made for Eric. Griffin must have been listening to it, even after he had made fun of Eric for it. What was it he said? "I have to tell you, buddy, very weak."

Why is he like that? Eric could never understand.

He was almost out the door, almost home free, when he had one last thought. Eric found a scrap of paper and a pen by the desk. He glanced out the window. There was no one around; Mary had wisely moved a few yards down the block, out of sight. He scribbled a few words on a piece of paper—"NOW

WE'RE EVEN"—and tucked it into the wooden box on the shelf.

Eric moved to the door, his hand squeezing the knob. Eric tilted his head, listening. Something had changed. It wasn't that he heard a sound, it was what he *didn't* hear: snoring.

He put his ear to the door, straining for any sound. *He should have snored by now,* Eric thought.

Then—*whooosh!*—the toilet flushed.

Mr. Connelly, two hundred seventy-five pounds of fat, mean ex-linebacker, had been sitting on his throne about fifteen feet away.

Eric made himself small behind the door.

Maybe he breathed, he couldn't be sure. Every muscle in his being, every nerve fiber, every cell, was focused on listening. He heard muffled sounds, water running, the clank of something against the wall, feet (slippers?) shuffling on the tile, the bathroom door opening. *Thump, thump, thump.*

The giant was not only awake. He was—*fee fi foe fum*—headed downstairs.

32
[door]

ERIC'S FIRST THOUGHT WAS GRIFFIN'S WINDOW. HE COULD climb onto the narrow portion of roof, figure out a spot to jump down without breaking his ankles, then hobble away. Eric wasn't crazy about that option. There had to be a better way.

The front door was at the bottom of the stairs. Eric's mind seized on that door, the gateway to his freedom. He could probably run down the stairs, noisy as anything, fling that door open, and go, man, go. Mr. Connelly wouldn't have time to react.

Eric crept out of the room. He listened from the

top of the stairs. Silence. Wait, no. The sound of a television—some sitcom show with phony patter and canned laughter. In his stocking feet, Eric took one step, then another. Fortunately, the top half of the stairs was obscured by a wall. But the wall gave way to an open banister about midway; heading down, Eric would be totally exposed.

He heard the shuffle of footsteps, the sound of a refrigerator opening, a glass set down on a table. Eric could picture huge Mr. Connelly, sitting at the kitchen table, elbows splayed, still in his tattered bathrobe.

A mental map of the house formed inside Eric's head. From the midpoint of the stairs, there was a clear view into the kitchen. That was the danger area. But it only lasted for about four steps. He took a deep breath. He decided that the best plan was to swiftly and silently walk down the stairs, don't hesitate, don't look around, don't so much as glance into the kitchen. Chances were, Mr. Connelly wouldn't even see him. The guy's face was probably buried in a bowl of Raisin Bran.

His heart thumped loudly, like a John Bonham drum solo thundering inside his chest. He began his descent. Eric made it to the bottom of the stairs when the father called, "Griff? When did you—?"

A jolt of adrenaline shot through Eric's body. He hit the door running, pulled open the inside door, pushed the outside screen door—*bang, clang*—but it didn't open. Panic set it. He heard the chair scrape across the linoleum floor, the brute heft of a man laboring to stand.

Locked, locked! There must be a switch, a thingy, a something to push or slide or . . .

There! The door swung open. Eric jumped the front porch steps and flew—absolutely flew—down the street. He turned left down one street, cut through a couple of yards, then turned down another street, then another, never looking back, just running hard, not caring who saw what, just putting as much distance between himself and the Connellys' as possible.

He found himself back at the little pocket park, the place where Mary had brought him. Eric collapsed on the bench, heaving to catch his breath, heart racing, mind a blur. He peered through the dense thicket of bushes, flipped open his cell, and punched numbers. Mary surely had seen him fleeing the house as if his hair were on fire. Hopefully she turned her phone off, breaking the connection, before turning it on again.

"Eric?"

"Mary!"

"You okay? What happened?"

"Yeah, yeah, I'm fine. Did he come after me?"

"No. He stood at the front door for a minute, looking baffled. Then he scratched his butt and went back inside."

Eric laughed, giddy and relieved.

That's when he finally noticed his stocking feet. *My sneakers!* Eric had left them in Griffin's room.

33
[kicks]

AVOIDING GRIFFIN CONNELLY WAS EASY ENOUGH FOR THE first half of the school day. Eric knew his habits, where his classes were, the pathways he traveled. But there would be no steering clear of him in the cafeteria. Eric vowed to himself that he wouldn't run. Whatever happened, happened. It wasn't much of a philosophy, but it was all Eric had. He was going to stand tall and stare Trouble in the eye. And if it smacked him in the mouth, well, Eric would figure out that part later.

He didn't see Griffin coming. Eric was already

seated across from Mary, trying to keep her from grabbing his dessert. Then Mary looked up and her eyes widened. Eric turned just as Griffin passed beside him, his elbow brushing the back of Eric's head ever so gently, like a whispered message. He kept walking, never looked back, didn't say a word. He didn't have to. His feet said it all.

Griffin Connelly was wearing Eric's sneakers.

Eric had to give Griffin credit: He had style. *Nice kicks,* Eric thought, figuring he'd probably never see those sneakers again—on his own feet, at least.

Griffin plopped down at his regular table, his back to Eric and Mary. Somehow they were dead even.

Cody sat with Griffin, like always. He was in the middle of telling a story, gesturing wildly with his hands, then smashing them together. Most likely reenacting some kind of NASCAR crash-up. Sinjay and Drew laughed; Griffin reached for a buttered roll on Marshall's lunch tray. Life went on. Down at the end of the table, Hakeem and Pat huddled together, talking quietly, somewhat apart. There was an empty chair, and it puzzled Eric for a moment. Then he realized whose it was: Hallenback's.

"Stop looking over there, will ya?" Mary complained.

"Sorry."

Two more girls had joined their table, Chantel and Sophie. When they sat down, Mary winked at Eric, silently mouthed the words, "Told you so." It had been her contention that their table would soon be filled with Misfit Toys—jack-in-the-boxes named Bruce, trucks with square wheels, boys who were too frail and skinny, girls whose looks didn't make the cut.

"Want to hang out after school today?" Eric asked.

"Sure," Mary said. "We have that science test tomorrow. I'm thinking about actually studying."

"You? Studying? I'll alert the media," Eric joked. Then he ventured, "We could go to the library and study together."

It was a deal.

Glancing around, Eric spied David Hallenback sitting alone in the far corner of the room. "Be right back," he told Mary.

David could see Eric coming from across the room. In response, he kept his head down, hunkered low over his lunch. *Trying to disappear,* Eric guessed.

"Hey," Eric greeted David.

The curly-haired boy looked up. His eyes were red-rimmed, his face ashen. Not much had changed since that first time Eric saw David, behind the middle school, shambling across the field. He was forever haunted and afraid. *Ketchup boy.*

"You okay?"

Hallenback looked up at Eric, and there was vacancy in his eyes. Not the old hatred. No spark of bitterness. Just defeat. He had been used and abused and now, obviously, once again banished from the table.

Eric tilted his head toward Mary. "There's room with us, if you want."

Hallenback glanced at the table, frowned, shook his head.

Eric shrugged. "You ever change your mind . . ."

Something caught his eye, a pin on Hallenback's shirt. "Hey, what's that pin? I never saw you wear it before."

David glanced down at the pin. It was in the shape of a baseball stadium. He shot a quick glance at Griffin, looked up at Eric. "I lent it to somebody. He finally gave it back this morning. It's from the stadium where the Mets play," David said, again looking down at the pin. "I got it on opening day."

"Sweet," Eric said. "Growing up in Ohio, I guess I became a Reds fan. I'm probably the only one in the whole school."

Hallenback considered that for a moment. "Now that you live here, you should switch to the Mets," he advised.

"I'll think about it," Eric said. "But it's hard to change loyalties, you know what I mean?"

Hallenback made a face that Eric couldn't quite read. *Whatever*. Eric didn't need to become friends with David Hallenback. He just needed, he realized, to be okay with himself.

At recess, Eric shot around on the basketball court. Pat and Hakeem joined him, along with a few other guys. "Are you trying out for the modified team this year?" Pat asked.

"You think I have a chance?"

"It's hard to say," Pat said, feeding a pass to Hakeem. "I think it's good to try out, you know, even if you don't make it, just so the coach sees you and learns your name. That's what my father says."

"It's mostly eighth-graders," Hakeem interjected. "Last year, I heard they took three seventh-graders, total."

Eric dribbled, spun, and dished to Pat.

"Open gym starts next week," Pat said. "We could check it out, you know. Guys just show up and shoot around. But the coach watches, I think. Real tryouts won't start for another two weeks."

Eric nodded. "Yeah, that sounds good."

Eric popped the ball out of Pat's hands, then dribbled to the far corner of the court. "Five, four—down by one, time is running out—three, two . . ." He hoisted up a long shot, an orange rainbow that ended with a metallic *swoosh* at the bottom of the net.

"Hayes makes the shot! Hayes makes the shot!" Eric called, his hands cupped around his mouth. "Bellport wins the championship! And the crowd . . . goes . . . wild!"

34

[coda]

TIME PASSED, BECAUSE THAT'S WHAT TIME DOES, IT'S A river that keeps pushing forward. November came, and with it, basketball season. Eric had miraculously survived the final cuts; he made the team, one of only two seventh-graders on the thirteen-member squad. It was one of his happiest days in a long time. His mother took him and Rudy out for enormous ice-cream sundaes to celebrate.

"Music helps," his father had once told him. And for Eric, that was so totally true. Through everything, he had his guitar and his amplifier. He played almost every night, headphones on, just fooling around, trying to figure out the chords to the songs in his head. That's what guitar meant to Eric. He was determined to learn the techniques, the difficult fingering and chord progressions, practice those scales until he could hammer each note without looking or even thinking. Because he knew there was a song trapped in his heart, an inchoate melody swelling in the dark, and he had to find a way to release it, to open that song up and cast it out into the world.

During those times, guitar in hand, Eric often thought of his father. It was when he felt most connected to him. They shared that love, undiminished, come what may. Eric had written more letters to his father, and mailed them, too. They weren't anything special. Nothing deep or particularly meaningful. But it was a beginning—a new beginning—and Eric was eager to discover where that might lead. He signed each letter the same. "Love, Eric." And maybe that was all that was necessary, that one true thought that said it all.

He thought about Griffin Connelly. They never talked anymore, never spoke of Eric's theft, or Griffin's new sneakers. It was like they made a silent pact.

Somehow it was all wiped clean, like chalk from a blackboard.

Eric figured that in the end, Griffin just got bored. They say people are supposed to forgive and forget, but in Griff's case, he just seemed to forget. So. Just like that, it was over. No final curtain. No big letters, THE END, flashing across the screen.

One day, not long ago, Eric walked down the hall and saw Griffin. He was with a new batch of friends, boys and girls Eric barely knew. Griffin was at the center, holding court, talking with that same cool confidence, beaming that golden smile. There was a girl by his side: Alexis Brown. They made a perfect couple.

Griffin didn't seem to see Eric. But Eric saw him— for he always kept a watchful eye on Griffin Connelly, never trusted him enough to feel completely safe. But for one split second, Eric saw Griff's eyes slide toward him. He saw Eric . . . and had no reaction at all. Eric was just another kid in the halls. A nobody. Not his enemy. Not his victim. Not his little side project, or his target.

That day, and every day since, nothing happened.

No "thing" at all. Eric kept walking, Griffin kept talking, both headed in different directions.

For the first time since he moved to Bellport, Eric wasn't a bully, a target, or a bystander. He was just Eric Hayes. A seventh-grade boy living on Long Island, trying to sort through a whole range of things, the teen years coming on hard, the challenges and confusions, maybe now on the verge of his first girlfriend, his first real kiss. All the while quietly hoping—in that place of the heart where words sputter and dissolve, where secret dreams are born and scarcely admitted—to score winning baskets for the home team. To take it to the hole and go up strong. Fearless, triumphant. The crowd on their feet.

His father in the stands, cheering.

Acknowledgments

THIS BOOK COULD NOT HAVE BEEN WRITTEN WITHOUT the help of many people, most especially: Chris Bergere, Jody Monroe, Andy Baker, Jen Steil, Bruce Oliver, and Matt Farnan. Thank you for opening your doors, answering questions, offering insights, and, in a few cases, reading early drafts.

To everyone at Feiwel and Friends, and most especially my editor and great pal, Liz Szabla: I feel like that guy who strolls under sunny skies and thinks, "Gosh, what a lucky fellow am I!" You've given me that feeling and I'm grateful for it, every single day.

While doing research for this book, different lines from Martin Luther King Jr. keep popping up in books, blogs, and Web sites—all speaking to what King termed, "the appalling silence." Though there are many salient quotes from King, one in particular had to find its way into this book: "In the end, we'll remember not the words of our enemies, but the silence of our friends."

Let's all make some noise.

GOFISH

JAMES PRELLER

What did you want to be when you grew up?
As a southpaw from Long Island, I dreamed of pitching for the New York Mets.

When did you realize you wanted to be a writer?
College, at Oneonta, New York. But in my teen years, I often wrote and kept a journal. I've found that it often helps to write things down, get words on a page, to discover what I'm truly thinking and feeling. We not only write what we know, we discover what we know . . . by writing.

What's your first childhood memory?
I vividly recall hiding under a table—and refusing to come out—when my grandmother visited from Queens Village. She was old and wrinkly, with pointy glasses, and wore a dead fox around her neck. Terrifying.

What's your favorite childhood memory?
I'm the youngest of seven children, so what I remember best— outside of the manic joy of Christmas—was the chatter and clatter and spilled milk of dinnertime together. It was like a

nightly hockey game, complete with thrown elbows, clutching, grabbing, and roughing penalties.

As a young person, who did you look up to most?
Do you mean I'm not a young person anymore? I had two older sisters and four older brothers—each remarkable and mysterious in his own way. Neil was the resident genius, who passed on to me his love of NYC and Bob Dylan; Bill was the motorhead, working in gas stations, and always the friendliest when I was little; John played guitar and had "Popeye" muscles; Al was, and still is, the stable easygoing one. And I was the pup, lapping it all up.

What was your worst subject in school?
English. Grammar, specifically.

What was your best subject in school?
PE and recess.

What was your first job?
Jones Beach concessions, West End Two. Great times. I just finished writing my first young adult novel, *Before You Go* (Spring 2012), and much of it borrows from that place and those times.

How did you celebrate publishing your first book?
Very, very quietly. Usually I'll buy a couple of CDs.

Where do you write your books?
I usually write at my computer, in the basement of my house. Someday I dream, like the rat in *The Tale of Despereaux*, of reaching the light, the light! These days I tend to write much of my first draft in longhand on a yellow legal pad.

Where do you find inspiration for your writing?
Since I usually write realistic fiction, I try to begin with an accurate understanding of a child's world, often by sitting in on various classrooms in my community. I have three children, ages 10, 11, and 17, so that helps me stay connected. I don't think you can examine something like "childhood" under a microscope, like a lab technician in a cold, white room. For a writer, you've got to feel it, and for whatever reason, I still remember.

When you finish a book, who reads it first?
It depends on the book. My editor, usually.

Are you a morning person or a night owl?
I'm a lunch and snack-time person. But as a father in a busy house, my strategy has been to try to outlast everyone. Then the house is mine, all mine! The older I get, the tougher that becomes.

What do you value most in your friends?
Tolerance, kindness. I also like a lively mind. *Interested* people are the most interesting.

Where do you go for peace and quiet?
Excuse me? Peace and quiet? What in the world are you talking about? Seriously: There's nothing like the solitary escape of reading a book. In many respects it's when we are most truly ourselves.

What makes you laugh out loud?
Will Ferrell in *Old School.*

What's your favorite song?
This changes over time. I'm a huge fan of all things Dylan, constantly rediscovering songs I thought I knew. But to name one song, this moment? Townes Van Zandt's "To Live Is to Fly." Thus the character in *Six Innings,* Dylan Van Zant. (I simplified the proper spelling of Zandt for the book.) Since I've been on iTunes, my most played song is "Love Minus Zero/No Limit" by Bob Dylan.

Who is your favorite fictional character?
Atticus Finch, *To Kill a Mockingbird.* I also like Frank Bascombe from Richard Ford's novels, and Rabbit—for his flaws and failures—from John Updike's series. It's interesting because both Frank and Rabbit are extremely flawed characters; I think it's our imperfections that make us interesting. People rarely want to read about a perfect character, though I suppose Atticus, as seen through Scout's eyes, comes very close to that.

What are you most afraid of?
Not being able to pay my bills, losing my house. In my line of work, it is a persistent concern.

What time of year do you like best?
Spring and autumn, the transitional seasons.

What's your favorite TV show?
New York Mets baseball.

If you were stranded on a desert island, who would you want for company?
My wife and children.

If you could travel in time, where would you go?
I'm most fascinated by the late '60s. And I guess I continue to return to that period, in my way, as a writer. It feels like those core childhood years have the deepest imprint. I'm forever going back, digging in the dirt.

What's the best advice you have ever received about writing?
Write from the heart. And . . . the day you send out a book submission, start another one. The worst thing you can do is sit around and wait for someone else's approval. Be true to yourself, that's another one.

What do you want readers to remember about your books?
That for a time they came along with me for a ride—and that they were in good hands.

What would you do if you ever stopped writing?
Edit. Books are my life's work, and I'd love to be able to play the role of an editor, help writers realize their talents, giving them the support and the opportunity that is so hard to come by. I think many of us are capable of great things, sometimes all it takes is someone in your ear, saying, "You can do this. I believe in you." So much of life is people putting limits on you, defining you, placing you in convenient boxes. It's so great when the possibilities open up. Part of being a great editor, with few exceptions, is giving up the dream of writing for yourself. The job is to serve the work, another writer's work, and I've never been able to give that up completely.

What do you like best about yourself?
Oh, dear, please, no. Unpretentiousness, I guess. I certainly
hate pretentiousness in other people. Anyone with a superior
attitude turns me off, completely.

What is your worst habit?
Does insomnia count? I think concentration is critical to per-
forming well in just about anything. It's why I think all of today's
talk about "multi-tasking" is malarkey. I often lack a laser-like
focus that is so essential to my job.

What is your best habit?
I read a lot.

**What do you consider to be your greatest
accomplishment?**
My life as a father.

Where in the world do you feel most at home?
Is this a trick question? At home! But outside of that, I'm always
happy on a hiking trail, somewhere in nature. On trips to Ireland I've felt connected in ways I can't fathom or explain. And I
love—even to this day—sitting out in centerfield during a ball
game (note: I used to play in a men's hardball league until very
recently), searching the sky for high-flying baseballs. I think it
connects me to something innocent and pure, chasing a round
white ball under a blue sky. I remain a boy at heart.

What do you wish you could do better?
I wish I could throw a real good live fastball.

What would your readers be most surprised to learn about you?

That I am so ordinary, so . . . unsurprising. On school visits, especially back in my early days, I was often troubled when teachers/students put "the visiting author" up on a pedestal. I'm not comfortable with that role. So then I found the solution: My task was to show them how utterly ordinary I was, that authors are no more special than doctors or architects or anyone else. I'm just another guy who works hard and does his best. That I'm . . . just like them. I think there's this idea that writers have to have these amazing, adventure-filled lives where big events happen. But I believe that writing (or *living*, for that matter) is really about how we *respond* to our lives, the richness and appreciation we bring to the ordinary.

Do you experience writer's block?

I don't believe in it, frankly. It's one more of those mystical things that writers are supposed to endure. I have a lunch-pail attitude to my job, since I don't have the luxury—in time or money—to sit around waiting for the muse to descend. I'm trying to pay the bills, you know? So I make things up. What I have learned—and what I will concede—is that there are times when the energy fails. (Writing, to me, requires great enthusiasm and energy.) I realized a while back that it was usually a sign that I was boring myself: That the story I was writing, or the specific scene, was flawed somehow. I was on the wrong path—and boring myself to tears. When the writing is right, I am fully engaged. When bored by my own words, I need to walk away and rethink things. Usually it means honing in a little closer to the rumblings of my own heart.

Do you use real life in your books?

Yes, all the time. My experiences, thoughts, feelings, dreams—my life is the primary source for everything I write. Could it be any other way? I can't imagine it. For *Six Innings*, I drew upon a lifetime of experiences. Yet surprises still came in the process of putting words on paper. One by one, different characters stepped forward. One boy, who soon served as the book's "play-by-play man," was very sick. To be honest, it was territory I resisted visiting. A place I didn't want to go. Because it was personal, something we experienced in our own family, something still raw and heartfelt, something that was not mine to own. It was my son Nick's journey, reinvented and relocated, yes, but in every meaningful way true to the core. You learn surprising things during a time of serious illness; unexpected "gifts" arrive in many forms. Oddly, you come away enriched, the heart bursting. And when you feel something that powerfully, well, that's always a good time to write.

Why did you write *Bystander*?

Too many times we see or read simplistic profiles of bullies and their targets. You know the clichés: the big, rough, unlikable lug who is, deep down, a coward at heart—picking on some wonderful, idealized child. Stand up to him and the bully runs away. Well, not quite. My research and my experience told me it was not that simple. Bullies are often popular, charismatic figures who select their victims with care and cunning, with a predator's sense of the weak and vulnerable. Also, it's important to realize that we are talking about behaviors, not labels that always apply. Kids who engage in bullying aren't simply "bullies." They are sons and friends and brothers and students and athletes and jokers and dreamers, etc. You can't reduce complex individuals down to these convenient categories. Bullying is an issue that affects and diminishes us all. That was the reason why I needed to call the book *Bystander*. Because that's where there's hope, in the silent majority that can make all the difference—if only we have the courage and conviction to step forward and learn to use our collective voices.

Why children's books?

Good question. I guess, like much in life, accident played a significant role. Out of college, knowing that I wanted to write . . . I became a waiter at Beefsteak Charlie's. A year later, I moved to Brooklyn and got a job as a junior copywriter at Scholastic, pulling down $12,500 a year, writing for the K–1 SeeSaw Book Club. My job was basically to read a ton of books and describe them to teachers and kids. It required two different voices. For teachers: "In this classic tale, H. A. Rey's mischievous monkey . . ." For students: "YIKES! That crazy monkey is in trouble again!" I met a lot of great books in that job, and the dream took hold. Anyone who works with children—or, for that matter, any parent, or anyone who has ever spent time with children—knows that kids give back. They respond, purely and directly. You get an immediate response from children that is so satisfying. Today I get fan letters that amaze me. At some point kids figure out that the book in their hands was written by a real person (not, as I once imagined, beamed down from another planet). Sometimes I'll walk into a classroom and can see it in a few sets of eyes: a reverence. I am not foolish enough to believe that they are in awe of me—I'm just a guy—but they love and respect books, and actually writing one seems like such an impossible, miraculous thing. My goal is to demystify the process. And in short order, after spending only a few minutes in my presence, the awe fades away. To be clear: I don't believe in the cult of celebrity, but I *am* still awed by books, still feel the wonder of stories, the life-changing power of words. I am grateful to have played a small role in that Great Conversation between reader and book.

It's the championship game,

and twenty-three boys are taking the field. Sam Reiser
is up in the booth, ready to call the play-by-play. Even
though he'd rather be joining his friends on the field,
he knows it'll be a great game to watch.

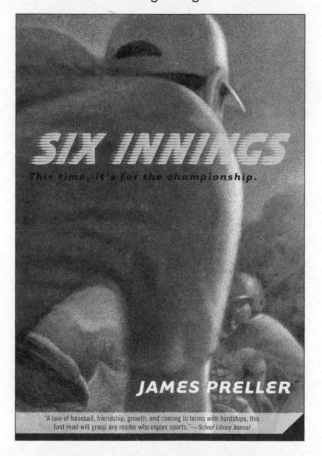

Join Sam and the players for all the action in

by **JAMES PRELLER**

・ 1 ・

Top of the First

	1	2	3	4	5	6	R	H	E
VISITORS	-								
HOME									

The one o'clock championship game is almost upon them, like a locomotive approaching from a great distance. The closer it gets, the larger it looms. And now here it is—that big train coming through.

The boys have already taken batting practice. They've warmed up and cooled down; chatted, joked, and poked, until, moments before the first pitch, they grow idle and contemplative.

Coach Reid brings the Earl Grubb's team together for a pregame talk. A muted shout breaks the quiet, hand claps and cheers erupt from inside the dugout. "Team!" they cry.

Up in the announcer's booth, Sam Reiser informs the crowd:

And now, please stand for our national anthem. . . .

Both teams hustle to the base paths, straddling the white lines that run from home plate to the respective foul poles. They take off their hats, hands on their hearts—Tyler Weinberg has to be reminded, and is, with a friendly whack on the head from Colin Sweeney—and they watch as the flag waves in a soft breeze. The anthem plays on a crackly sound system. And now at last, it's time for the game. Northeast Gas & Electric, the home team by virtue of a superior regular-season record, takes the field.

Dylan Van Zant stands about ten feet from home plate, timing his swing to Nick Clemente's warm-up pitches. Clemente throws nothing but fastballs that explode in catcher Travis Green's glove. *Pop, pop, pop.*

"Balls in!" Green cries out.

The fielders toss their practice baseballs in lazy arcs toward the home-team dugout along the first-base line.

"Coming down!" Green hollers.

The smooth, dark-skinned shortstop, Justin Pinkney, glides over to second base, backed up by the pint-size second baseman, Billy Thompson. Clemente snaps off a half-hearted curveball that floats in like a helicopter. Green snares it deftly, rises, and fires a laser to second base. *Strong arm,* Dylan notes admiringly, *great catcher.*

The umpire, bulky and dressed in dark blue, calls, "Come on. Play ball!"

From his seat in the announcer's booth, behind and above

home plate, Sam Reiser feels his heartbeat quicken. *Play ball.*
He leans into the microphone and pushes the black button.

**Leading off for Earl Grubb's Pool Supplies, today's
starting pitcher, Dylan Van Zant. . . .**

As his name is announced, Dylan looks down the third-
base line to Mr. Reid, who is stationed in the coach's box.
The skipper claps his hands, nods. "Get us started, Dilly."

Dylan has already decided to take the first pitch. It doesn't
matter where the ball goes, Dylan won't swing. He wants to
see Clemente's fastball, up close and personal. Watch his motion, look for the release point—but mostly, try to relax. Get
rid of the bees that are buzzing in his brain. Because here he
stands, playing for the championship. How cool is that?

Dylan takes a fastball down the pipe for strike one.

It has begun.

Clemente has the unsettling habit of grunting with each
pitch. He's like a bull in a pen, eager to break loose. *Snort,
snort, fliiiing.* Already at five feet, ten inches and 170 pounds,
Clemente is colossal for a seventh-grader. Scary as all get-go
and he knows it. Clemente works quickly. In seconds he's
back on the rubber, charging into his delivery; he plays like
his hair is on fire.

Dylan swings and misses at a chest-high fastball,
corkscrewing his wiry frame into the earth. *Late,* Dylan
thinks. *Way late.* He steps out of the box, takes a breath,
feels the electric undercurrent from the packed bleachers.

Clemente glowers from the mound, hoofing the dirt with his cleats.

The count is no balls, two strikes. No one out. No runners on base. The game has scarcely begun, but already Clemente has set the tone. He is going to work fast and throw gasoline. His every move an act of defiance, a dare that says, "Hit me if you can."

Down two strikes, Dylan inches his fingers up the bat handle. *Fast to the ball*, he tells himself. Protect the plate. No matter what, don't go down looking. There's nothing worse than striking out with the bat on your shoulders.

Clemente, square-shouldered and built like a soda machine, rocks back into his windup. His hands come together before his chest, pump back over his head, the left knee lifts up as he pivots, pushes off the rubber on a thick right leg, drives toward the plate with maximum force. *Uhhhmmmgh.*

The pitch is just ridiculous. A curve that acts as if it were dropped from the sky. One moment the ball is right there, then it isn't. Gone, vanished, like it fell into a manhole.

Dylan swings and misses. The home-plate umpire signals strike three. Green zips the ball back to Clemente, who sneers with satisfaction.

Batting second, Nando Sanchez. . . .

The name on his birth certificate is Armando, after a grandfather back on the island. Everyone calls him Nando. And he is very fast. Everything Nando does, from eating waffles to fielding grounders, is restless and quick. He swings in short, choppy strokes—a slap hitter, not a power threat. "We will work with that," his father announced one day. "Speed never slumps. Hit the ball on the ground and fly, Nando, fly."

Thin and undersized, Nando bats with an exaggerated crouch, presenting the pitcher with a small strike zone. He takes the first two pitches high for balls. Clemente steps off the mound, angrily slams the ball into his glove. Clemente's fury surprises Nando, almost frightens him. Clemente grunts and fires another pitch.

"Strike one!" the umpire calls.

Hot stuff, thinks Nando, *caliente*. Nando steps out of the box, wipes his lips with the back of his sleeve, tightens his batting gloves, and eyes Coach Reid as he goes through the signs. Reid touches his hat, the indicator, then goes to his belt buckle. Nando understands: *Bunt*. The alert third baseman, Angel Tatis, also seems to sense the possibilities. He creeps in, bent low, his glove licking the tips of the grass.

Nando squares early, showing the bunt, bat held loosely at chest level. The pitch comes in high and tight. Nando falls away, instinctively using his bat for protection. Somehow he manages to bunt the ball foul as he collapses to the ground. Strike two.

"That's okay, Nando! You're okay!" his father shouts from the stands. "Two strikes now, Nando! You've got to protect!" Nando turns to see his father, mother, maternal grandparents, two brothers, and baby sister crowded together in their seats. They have come to watch Nando play in the great championship game. Not watch, no, they've come to cheer—wildly, enthusiastically, passionately. Nando hopes to make them proud on this day, not seeming to realize that it's already been accomplished, long ago. He focuses back on the pitcher.

Clemente stares with reptilian eyes, cold and lifeless. He won't waste a curveball on a weak hitter like Nando. It will be a steady diet of fastballs until Nando proves he can catch up to one.

"You must earn the pitcher's respect," Mr. Sanchez told his son many times. "He has to get *you* out, not the reverse, *comprende*, Nando? That's why you must have confidence. Go to the plate like you own it, like you own the whole field. Swing the bat and make him respect you!"

Nando doesn't stand a chance. Strike three cuts the outside corner, or at least that's how the umpire sees it, and his is the only opinion that matters. It's not a debate club. To Sam's eyes, the ball looked six inches wide of the plate. Tough break for Nando. The first blown call of the day. It wouldn't be the last.

In the Pool Supplies dugout, all the players push forward at once, eager to watch this next matchup. Branden Reid might be the team's hottest hitter, sturdy and broad-shouldered. More than that, he has become one of the leaders of the team, the kid everyone respects. If Branden can't hit Clemente, what chance did anyone else have?

A loud, guttural voice calls out, "Let's go, kiiiiiiid!"

Sam instantly recognizes the voice, for it can only be

Mike Tyree. Sam leans forward to get a better look into the Pool Supplies dugout. At that same instant, Mike returns Sam's gaze, as if they were connected by an invisible thread.

It had happened dozens of times before. It was, in fact, how they became friends, back in Mrs. Geller's first-grade class. It took one wordless exchange—right after Aaron Foley threw up during a math lesson. Spectacularly. Gloriously. Voluminously.

Aaron Foley, short and stocky with a squished-in face that reminded Sam of an English bulldog, did more than toss his cookies. No, Aaron *projected* his vomit across the room, spewing his insides as if fired from a cannon, a thunderous blast of wet barf splattering onto the tile floor.

No one spoke. No one moved.

Mrs. Geller at last motioned to Janice Dingum. "Better fetch Joe the janitor. Tell him to bring a mop"—she paused a beat—"and a large bucket."

At that precise moment, Sam glanced up only to catch Mike staring back at him, his face a mixture of mirth and horror, delight and stunned awe. Somehow each boy knew how the other felt, knew it *exactly*. A telepathy that focused on a single word: *Recess.*

Mrs. Geller asked Austin Hayes to escort Aaron to the nurse's office, a request that Austin accepted with reluctance. The teacher then shooed everyone out onto the playground until Joe arrived with that mop.

On the jungle gym, the boys snickered, recounting Foley's

heroic hurl. Extra recess! Good old Aaron Foley! That's how Sam and Mike began their friendship, sealed with a simple exchange, a look across a silent (but foul-smelling) distance.

Mike will try to sneak away to visit Sam later if he gets a chance. It almost feels wrong that he's on the field, while Sam—the better player—is stuck up there. Mike checks the stands and wonders: *Will they come?* His parents miss so many of his games. But this one is different. This time, it means something to Mike.

He remembers that it was late when he got dropped off after the final regular-season game. The NBA playoffs were on television. Mike waited, still in uniform, watching, mildly interested. The station broke for a commercial.

"So? How'd you do?" Mr. Tyree asked.

"We won," Mike answered.

But Mike's father noted, "I asked how did *you* do."

"Pretty good," Mike said. "I walked, stole a base, and scored. I made a nice play at third base. I like playing the infield."

"No hits?" his father asked.

Mike didn't have an answer for that.

The commercials were finished, the game was back on. The conversation, Mike knew, was nearly over. "We clinched a spot in the championship game," Mike announced. "It's on

Saturday." Mike's head pivoted from his mother to his father. "It would be great if you can, you know, come to the game."

"You know that Saturdays are tough," his mother commented. "We'll see."

Which to Mike's ears meant one thing: If your sister Candace has an AAU basketball game—and doesn't she always?—then you're out of luck. Because there already was a star athlete in the Tyree family. And her name wasn't Mike.

That's two up and two down for Clemente.
Next to the plate, catcher Branden Reid. . . .

Other boys in the dugout pick up Mike's battle cry. "Come on, kiiiiiiiid," they exhort. More calls come from the lively dugout, hoots of encouragement. Branden Reid eyes Clemente as he walks to the plate, cool as a three-bean salad.

He pulls the first pitch foul down the third-base line, forcing his father to leap out of the way. Coach Reid pulls a handkerchief out of his pocket and waves it. "I surrender, I surrender," he comically gestures to the crowd.

The scattered laughter irritates Branden. He likes his dad and everything, but this isn't the time for clowning around.

Up in the booth, Sam pops a peanut M&M into his mouth. He thinks, *Quick bat. Not too many guys can pull Clemente's fastball.* It comes as no consolation that, in fact, Sam himself is one of the few guys with hands fast enough to do it. Sam loves facing fastball pitchers.

Down on the field, Nick Clemente challenges Branden with another fastball, but this time in a better spot. High and inside, right above the crook of the elbow. Branden barely manages to foul it back off the screen.

Down two strikes, Branden still feels confident. He knows he can catch up to the fastball. He feels loose, relaxed. His bad arm doesn't bother him when he swings the bat. It only hurts when he throws. Branden calls time, steps out of the box, if only to mess with Clemente, who snorts with impatience. All Clemente knows is *now, now, now*. He's pent up, eager to kick down walls. So Brandon dawdles, taps his cleats free of imaginary mud, casually picks a piece of sand out of the corner of his eye.

He got Dylan on an 0–2 curveball, Branden figures. He prepares himself for it, thinking, *Weight back, hands back*. But Clemente comes with a fastball, a pea at the knees. Branden's eyes widen, he swings through the pitch. Branden looks back at the catcher's glove in disbelief. He got beat by a fastball. *Damn, just missed it.*

In baseball, scouts refer to the five tools: speed, glove, arm, power, and the ability to hit for average. It is rare for one player to excel in all five areas. Branden Reid, however, possesses a sixth tool, amnesia, the art of forgetting. Baseball is, after all, a game of failure. The only thing that a player can influence is the *next* play, the *next* at-bat. The strikeouts, the errors, the defeats? Ancient history, best forgotten, or at least pushed aside. So Branden hustles back into the dugout, pulls on the catching gear, and steps back into the sun.

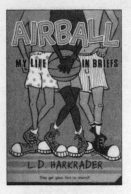